PROJECT MOONBASE

JC Crumpton Kevin Findley Neal Privett
John Holmes Aaron Bittner

PRO SE PRESS

PRO SE ⚖ PRESS

PROJECT MOONBASE
A Pro Se Productions Publication

We Take Care of Our Own by JC Crumpton
Lunar Ruse by Kevin Findley
The Mummies of Tara al Bay by Neal Privett
Missing by John Holmes
Halloran's Mine by Aaron Bittner
Editing by AJ Johnson, Tommy Hancock, Taylor Bray, Tara Dugan, David Gilmore, Kathy Samuels

Cover by Larry Nadolsky
Book Design by Antonino Lo Iacono & Marzia Marina
New Pulp Logo Design by Sean E. Ali
New Pulp Seal Design by Cari Reese

Pro Se Productions, LLC
133 1/2 Broad Street
Batesville, AR, 72501
870-834-4022

editorinchief@prose-press.com
www.prose-press.com

PROJECT MOONBASE
Copyright © 2017 Each Respective Author

CONTENTS

WE TAKE CARE OF OUR OWN

By
JC Crumpton

"In my opinion, sir," Chief Carter said into his mic after thumbing the channel, so that only his supervisor and the system recording could hear, "you're a damn fool."

He watched as the ensign's suit stood up from behind the control station. The way his limbs jerked, overcompensating for the moon's weaker gravity, indicated to him that the boy was getting ready to let loose with one of his tirades. Not only did he have to deal with the sudden work stoppage because of some anomalous graviton readings, but he also had to play nice and deal with the snot-nosed Ensign Theodore Rae and his inane ramblings.

Chief Carter continued reviewing the latest findings from the Digger on his heads-up display. Calculus and trigonometry had never been his strongest subjects in training, but his experience with structural integrity and station design more than compensated for any ignorance. And in spite of that experience, the ensign never let him forget who had the better education and superior rank.

"None of the physicists or civil engineers at Alpha Base mentioned anything about odd readings in their reports this morning, Chief," Ensign Rae said as he bumbled over to the Digger where Chief Carter stood with two of his crew.

"I don't know about that, sir," the chief explained while he tapped his supervisor's email address into his comm-pad to send the latest readings from the Digger."This is just what the machine is reporting. In my experience, I would suggest shutting this operation down until we can get a better fix on what is happening."

The link remained silent for a few breaths, and then Chief Carter saw that the ensign had opened up the comms for the entire hull maintenance tech team."Chief," Ensign Rae began,"I have a structural engineering degree from Illinois Institute of Technology and have been admitted into the Advanced Astro-engineering program at Stanford for this coming fall."

Chief Carter waited for the other shoe to fall, and the ensign never disappointed."Do you have credentials like these?"

"No, sir."

"Then you probably don't understand the math behind the readings about which you are so concerned."

"Not completely, sir."

"Are you a physicist, Chief?"

Carter snorted."Not in the slightest, sir."

"Then how would you even know what a graviton reading looks like?" the ensign said."Leave the heavy thinking to people like me."

Chief Carter waved at the Digger."Because that's what the console says."

"Don't get flippant with me, Chief." The ensign tried to move his right hand across his body in a motion meant to signify an end to the conversation, but it looked more like some child's animatronics giant teddy bear getting ready to begin some broad, exaggerated dance."I would suggest that you and your team get back to work clearing out this section of tunnel and getting the hull plates set in place."

Exhaling slowly after he muted his mic, the chief tried to relax and control the shaking in his hands. Red warning lights flashed on the Digger's main screen, indicating the presence of an energy source which had an unknown stability. He went over the numbers again quickly. The density of the next section of rock could not be determined, and the chief didn't want to break through into something that could either delay the project even more or be dangerous to any of his crew.

They had started late on the job of building the first darkside lunar base after the negotiations between the United States' Department of Defense and the United Nations had stalled six months ago over a disagreement in the terminology of the neutrality treaties attached to the moon and near-Earth objects. Administrative bureaucracy couldn't get the project back on track in time, and even after it had been green-lighted, Chief Carter wasn't able to bring his crew in for another three weeks.

The chief licked his lips and opened the link."How many low-gravity construction projects have you worked on yourself, sir?"

"I fail to see the relevance, Chief."

"I'm just wondering, sir," he answered,"how many projects outside the Earth's atmosphere and gravity well you or any of your professors have physically worked on, rather than just theorizing about them."

"If you continue, Chief," said the ensign, his voice coming across the link clipped and strained,"I will be forced to write you up for belligerence."

"I understand, sir." Another warning signal sounded from the Digger, and the chief pulled it to his HUD. The gravity fluxes had increased."However, the crew standing in front of you has over fifty combined years of practical application of all those fancy theories you've read about and had classes on."

"This is your last warning, Chief."

"Then I would like it recorded in the duty log that I am following this order under duress and against my experienced judgment."

"Noted, Chief," the ensign snapped."Now get digging."

Six weeks ago, the Construction Battalion received orders to begin excavating the tunnels beneath the Alden Formation. After they broke ground, Chief Carter and his crew of four hull technicians came in to install permanent polypropylene bulkheads so that atmosphere could be pumped in and military and scientific personnel could start populating the base. But the project hit a snag about a klick beneath the surface under one of the eight spokes that radiated out from a central shaft leading back up to the domed surface.

He stared at the Digger's console and used his gloved hand to tap repeatedly on his faceplate. It recommended not proceeding further due to unrecognized energy signatures. Chief Carter had told Skeeter to call for a quantum engineer from the surface. What he got instead was his immediate supervising officer.

Seven months fresh out of Annapolis hadn't mellowed out the boy's arrogance one little bit. And Carter did not know how much more incompetence he could tolerate. Still awkward in the lower gravity, Ensign Theodore Rae's form half-stumbled, half-fell down the corridor back to the safety of the mobile comm-cen so he could monitor their progress from its protected atmosphere.

After the ensign had finished retreating to the comfort of the MCC, Chief Carter toggled the link to his crew only. He waited a few moments before they all noticed on their HUDs that they were on the private channel.

Chief Carter nodded. He licked his lips, which always seemed to dry out quicker after breathing the canned air for a few days."I don't like this one bit, guys."

"We're with you, Chief," Skeeter piped in up."This smells like a major screw-up."

He turned his left hand top to bottom, signifying a shrug to his men and those that had experience working in EVA suits."I know you like working in these Z-series suits because of their pliability, but this doesn't feel right. We're all going to wear the heavy suits."

"I hate them damn D-Vac EVA things, Chief," Weezer protested."They're a bitch to get in and out of. The shift's half over by the time you get started workin'." From the hills of West Virginia, Chief Carter knew that Petty Officer Second-Class Frances Weasley had come from a long line of coal miners. He had this excavation job in his genes.

"My grandfather didn't use special equipment back under the Appalachians," Weezer complained."I don't see why we need to waste half our shift gettin' in-'n'-out of them things."

Skeeter's sharp laugh came across the comms."That's because they were too pickled from moonshine or too busy porking their hillbilly sister."

Weezer shifted and stepped away from the Digger, his face reddening beneath the faceplate, but Carter put his hand on the young mech driver's arm."Take it easy, Weezer. He didn't mean anything mean by it."

Nodding, Weezer turned back to the Digger, but Skeeter called after him,"I know you wouldn't bone your sister, Weezer. No hard feelings?"

Weezer only grunted."Besides," Skeeter added,"I've seen your sister."

"That's enough of that, Skeeter," Carter snapped before Weezer could do more than spin around."We've got a job to finish." He looked over at the rest of his crew."I know. But I need to worry about your safety before your comfort." He switched over to the open channel and began recording audio."You heard Ensign Rae. We need to double-time it to get this job back on schedule. That means if we're going to break through this next section against the recommendation of the Digger, then we are going to be properly equipped to handle any unknown event."

Several of his crew touched their helmets with their fingertips in the equivalent to an EVA suit nod."Yes, Chief," a few muttered.

Forty minutes later, Chief Carter made sure everyone had their Deep Vacuum EVA suits on properly and were all jacked into the proper comm channels. They made their way through the sections they had already completed, lumbering slowly like a line of armored giants marching to some unknown war. He didn't like making them wear the heavier equipment, but this whole thing felt like it had the potential to explode into a storm.

They came to the end of the finished tunnels and stepped into the corridors of raw rock. Chief Carter asked Weezer to go over to the Digger so he could get it warmed up and ready to chew through the next section.

"I ain't likin' this, Chief."

"What's up, Weezer?" the chief asked.

The man turned his left hand up and over."The readin's have changed, and the SI is still recommendin' that we don't dig any deeper."

Chief Carter coughed and started to drop a few words that wouldn't go over in a review of the audio very well, but he remembered they were recording."Sometimes I wish these semi-intelligent processors were fully intelligent."

He turned back to the Digger and motioned Weezer forward. Ensign Rae had positioned the MCC at the end of the completed section where the seals would adhere to the polypropylene bulkheads and he could watch them in comfort.

"Move it forward, Weezer," the chief commanded."Let's chew

through this and get back up topside for some R&R."

"You got it, Chief," Weezer said over the channel."Hammerin' down."

Even though the vacuum couldn't carry sound waves, Chief Carter imagined the machine growling as it bit into the solid rock in front of it. But he felt the tremors that rumbled through the ground and up into the metal of the D-Vac suits. It set his teeth on edge like he had bit onto a piece of vibrating metal. He started to sweat inside his suit. In all its infinite wisdom, the Navy issued undergarments of slicker material to each sailor to wear next to their skin under the suits. He wondered what senator or former president had a controlling interest in the industry that made them for and sold them to the government at an exorbitantly jacked up price. He always believed that to be the reason they didn't just wear old-fashioned cotton t-shirts that could soak up the perspiration.

His link to the Digger chimed in his ear and another warning came up on his HUD advising him to hold position and evaluate the next six meters of rock. He motioned for Weezer to shut the machine down and waved HT Second-Class Myri Guzman over.

"Yes, Chief." Her northern Mexican accent, straight from Guadalajara, always sounded to him as if she could break out into song any second.

The message indicator popped up on his HUD, telling him that Ensign Rae was busy trying to connect with him, but he tagged it for later retrieval."Punch this with the GPR. I want to see if it can reveal anything beyond this next section yet."

"Sure thing." Guzman touched her hand to the top of her faceplate."But I'm just going to tell you. The SeaBee techs couldn't find anything either."

The chief tapped the side of his helmet twice. I know."I just want to be thorough. No room for error. This is unknown territory."

She had already started walking back to the materials shed at the beginning of the raw portion of tunnel. He could see the ensign pacing back and forth inside the MCC, waving his hands around in broad sweeps. Guzman tapped her helmet once, and he knew the officer had opened a private channel to her. He obviously didn't like what she had to say because he continued his strides and had turned red in the face.

Chief Carter tabbed open a private channel and asked Guzman what that had all been about, but she just turned her hand top to bottom and back. Beats me.

She walked up to the wall five minutes later with the portable ground-penetrating radar generator and grabbed both controls with her gloves."No guts. No glory."

"No glory without guts," several of his men answered over the open comm channel.

Guzman activated the machine. The chief watched the screen over her right shoulder and grimaced when it came back with nothing but static. His message indicator pinged again, and he let out a long sigh before answering.

"Yes, sir?"

As strained and as high-pitched as Ensign Rae's voice squealed across the channel, Chief Carter wondered just how long ago the boy had gone through puberty."I thought I gave you a direct order to punch through this section, Chief. Correct me if I'm wrong, but did I not give you specific instructions that we were to do our utmost to get this project back on schedule?"

"Yes, you did, Ensign."

"Then why did you stop the Digger to take yet another reading with the GPR?"

Chief Carter turned around to his men with his back to the MCC."Just following standard safety protocols, sir. We needed another reading to make sure we wouldn't be breaking across any fault or unstable seam. If we didn't follow USNA Navy regulations on this, we would have to file it in an Exceptions Report DOC-1USNA, sir. And if we did that, then the review could put the operation behind even more."

He waited for a few seconds, and when Ensign Rae only answered him with silence, the chief asked,"Would you like for me to fill out an Exceptions Report, sir?"

He heard the link click off. The ensign hadn't even demeaned himself to respond. Chief Carter motioned with his right hand. Oh, well.

"Crank her up, Weezer," he said into his mic.

"You got it, Chief," the driver replied."No glory without guts."

"No guts. No glory," the rest of the crew responded.

The Digger rumbled to life, and it inched forward. The dull gray bit immediately spun up so fast that the grooves and sections blurred into a haze as it chewed into the rock face. Sonic generators emitted focused beams of sound into the rock, vibrating the material to a point the Digger poured through it like water breaking before a keel. Smoke and dust mixed together in the hole dug out of the wall, powdered bits of debris and stone.

By the time the machine had mined through three meters of rock, the entire wall disintegrated and crumbled into pebbles on the floor. Where the wall of stone should have been, a wall of opaque, blue energy crackled and separated the tunnel from what appeared to be an empty, round chamber on the other side of the shimmering curtain.

Chief Carter motioned for Weezer to cut the engine, shouting quick commands through the open channel. As soon as Weezer shut down the Digger, the energy field appeared to bulge briefly, covering the entire drill bit before it contracted into a spinning blue ball. They all stared at the rotating energy. Chief Carter felt his stomach tighten. He barked into his mic and ordered his crew to retreat back up the tunnel.

Before any of them moved, the ball of energy expanded faster than any of the sailors could react. It swelled from the ball barely a meter in diameter to fill the worksite nearly instantaneously. The sudden expansion hurled Chief Carter away from the room, slamming him into the wall before the first bend in the tunnel. Vibrations shuddered through the ground and into his D-Vac suit, and pieces of stone plinked against his faceplate. Chief Carter rolled his head over, staring in disbelief at where cracks radiated up the corridor sides from where the energy pulse had driven the Digger into the wall a few meters away. Debris from where it had shattered the rock had been thrown at the chief.

He pushed himself to his feet and lumbered back to the dig site. The energy had shrunk back into the spinning ball, suspended a meter off the floor and throwing off an occasional blue spark. The sparks raced through strange patterns carved into the floor like mice in a maze, moving though through some Escher-designed warren of corridors.

Leaning against the edge of the new chamber, he thumbed his mic open."Sound off."

One by one his crew reported in except for one, and from the wreckage, he feared what he would learn. Skeeter cleared his throat and walked towards the chief from the other side of the Digger.

"Sorry, Chief," he began."Weezer didn't make it."

"Damn it!" Chief Carter shouted, slamming his fist against the wall and freeing a few bits of debris that tumbled slowly until coming to a rest near his feet. He stared at the pebbles and slowed his breathing until he could no longer hear his own heartbeat in his ears.

Ensign Rae stumbled down the hall in his own D-Vac suit. The young officer looked strained through his faceplate, sweat slipping down his forehead and across the bridge of his nose.

Pushing himself away from the wall, Chief Carter turned towards the ensign and started in his direction. He could still hear the rushing of blood in his head and knew that he was about to commit an offense for which he would very likely be drummed out of the Navy and thrown into a dark brig for a very long time. But he couldn't find it in himself to care until Guzman called him on the crew channel.

"Chief!" her voice broke through his intense concentration on Ensign Rae.

"What is it, Guzman?"

He looked around and saw the young woman standing next to the opening into the chamber. The whirling ball of energy shed blue light in shimmering waves over one side of her suit, casting a long shadow that reached down the tunnel.

She held her right hand palm up and turned it back down quickly."I don't know, Chief. But it ain't good."

"What do you mean?" he asked, tapping the side of his helmet with two fingers.

"I can't raise topside to get a medical unit down here."

Chief Carter stopped in the middle of the rubble scattered across the corridor. After thumbing through various channels without a response, he switched to Extra Low Frequency and broadcast there, hoping the longer ELF waves could punch through the rock to the surface. A feedback squelch blasted through his earpiece and forced him to reach out to regain his balance. Nothing but static answered his repeated calls.

His crew all staggered or limped back to edge of the chamber. Ensign Rae waved his arms back and forth standing in front of the chief and then the other crew members one by one, but they all tapped the sides of their helmets and shook their heads. Chief Carter opened the crew channel.

The indicator on his HUD flashed to let him know the ensign was pinging away, trying to get anyone to answer him. Chief Carter started to respond, but the sparks racing through the patterns carved into the floor began to coalesce in the center of the chamber and drip up into the rotating ball. The energy whirled about like an opaque tornado of blue light and dust.

"Skeeter?"

"Yeah, Chief?" the man answered.

"Is your suit cam working?"

Before Skeeter answered, the ball expanded into a broad pillar three meters across and reached from the floor to the ceiling.

"Rolling, Chief," Skeeter said.

"Good."

"This is going to win me a golden statue."

Chief Carter finally opened the channel to the ensign. But before he could say anything, Ensign Rae shouted,"Clear this chamber, Chief. This is a new discovery, and the last thing we need is for you or your crew to be screwing things up before the scientists get here to study this phenomenon."

Studying the pillar of light and trying not to look at him, Chief Carter asked the ensign,"You've heard of those gravitons, right, sir?"

"Don't be a wiseass, Chief," the ensign said."They're particles emitted from a wormhole or singularity. Sometimes they can be detected as stray objects racing through the solar system. So? Did you need me to help you out with this?"

Chief Carter nodded at the pillar."Because I believe that is where the energy readings were coming from and why the rock seemed more dense before we breached this chamber."

"I didn't know you were a physicist, Chief."

The chief put his hand palm up and turned it over."Just a hypothesis, sir."

He turned to his men."Skeeter."

"Yes, Chief?"

"You and Wilson double-time it back to the locker and get the pulse rifles and all the frags you can carry."

"Aye, Chief," Skeeter said. He and Wilson turn and skipped down the hall as fast as their suits and the lower gravity let them.

"What do you think you're doing, Chief?" Ensign Rae asked, waving down the hall after the two men."You are not authorized to carry weapons on a construction job."

Carter tapped his helmet with his gloved hand."This isn't a construction project anymore, sir."

"Then what is it?" the ensign sneered.

"This is a defensive countermeasure."

"A what?"

Chief Carter pointed a finger in the ensign's direction."Listen, sir. I can either take the time to explain this to you in simple enough terms that you can understand, or you can just pick up a weapon and prepare to repel invaders."

"What…?" Ensign Rae began.

"I don't have time, sir. Either man up, or better yet, hustle back up topside and warn the base. Get a company of marines down here."

"How do you know this, Chief?"

He held up his terminal display so the ensign could see it for himself."Because from the moment we breached the chamber, comm-links to the surface have been down. And this field of energy has been emitting regular pulses that are growing closer and closer together. If I'm right, it's getting ready to be awfully crowded in here when an Einstein-Rosen Bridge opens on this spot."

"Maybe they're just explorers, Chief," the officer suggested.

"Sure, Ensign," Chief Carter said."Explorers contacting another species always feel it best to visit them by announcing themselves secretly."

The young man clicked off his comm unit, and Chief Carter sighed inwardly. He flipped through the channels again, trying to get a signal through to the surface, but even with the power turned up, he knew he wouldn't be able to reach anyone. His HUD readings told him everything he needed to know. Some burst of energy had overwhelmed all the sensors throughout the entire tunnel system.

He checked his suit readings and pulled those of his crew up on his HUD, making sure that they all still functioned. His back, along the spine between his shoulder blades, ached from where he had been slammed into the wall. The suit couldn't work fast or hard enough to filter out the stench of his own sweat, and the acrid odor forced him to breathe through his mouth. He hoped the waste reclamation system still functioned and that his body wouldn't be found later with him having crapped his pants.

His earpiece chirped, and he looked back up the tunnel to see Skeeter and Wilson loping down the tunnel carrying several pulse rifles each and leading a squad of four armed and armored marines. Skeeter and Wilson pulled up in front of the chief while the marines fanned out to either side of the pillar of energy, with their rifles aimed and ready.

"Where'd you find your friends, Wilson?" Chief Carter asked the junior crew member, just two months out of "A" school.

Wilson fumbled with the loading mechanism on the pulse rifle. The young man, born and raised on a lunar outpost and used to spending much of his time in EVA suits, obviously felt flustered because he started moving his hands and arms in the signals meant to simplify communication in hard vacuum. Carter stepped over to him and put his hand on Wilson's shoulder. When he looked up, Chief Carter put his own hand over his sternum for a second before lowering it palm down to his waist. Calm/center yourself. Slow down.

The young man tapped his helmet twice. Understood. He flipped on his comms."They had just arrived on routine patrol, Chief. They said the energy surge knocked out all their comms as well as the elevator."

"Thank you, son," Carter said. He turned and looked at the squad leader, nodding as the marines filed into the room.

He opened a wide channel on his comms."I want everyone to charge up and fan out around this chamber. Your field of fire will be centered on the bridge opening. Do not position where you can hit a friendly accidently should you miss. And ignite your IR probes. We don't want anyone mistaking us for hostiles."

Beside him, Guzman charged her rifle and joined the marines in the room, her helmet turning back and forth between the chamber and the tunnel where Ensign Rae paced back and forth.

Chief Carter powered up his own weapon and stepped into the chamber with Skeeter and Wilson flanking him on either side.

The channel with the ensign opened, and Carter heard the officer's ragged voice between gasps as if the man were about to hyperventilate."You will stand down, Chief. And that is an order." He watched through the edge of his faceplate as Ensign Rae walked towards one of the marines."You will stand down, marine. Do you hear me?"

Chief Carter chinned the command channel open and asked,"Did you spend any time studying military tactics at the Academy, sir?"

"You know I did, Chief," Rae said."What does that have to do with the fact that you are all disregarding a direct order from the ranking officer? You will all be written up."

Stifling a snicker, Chief Carter said,"Then you should know, sir, that what we have here is an attempt to establish a beachhead."

The channel remained silent, and the Ensign stopped his progress into the room and started to slowly back out slowly. He coughed once, and his voice cracked when he tried to say something. The sound of him swallowing and clearing his throat came clearly through the earpiece.

"Then we need to fall back," Rae began."We need to…um…form up in a more defensible position."

"No time, Ensign," Chief Carter said."We sure could use some help down here, though. If you want to get back up and try to repair the elevator so you can warn the base, that would go a long way to saving lives."

Before the ensign could respond, the blue light shimmered, deepening in color. A long metal tube held by two gloved hands came out of the column of energy, seeming to materialize from nothing but the light. Without thinking, Chief Carter charged forward and threw himself at whatever was coming through. The moment his forearms contacted something solid and pushed it back into the beam, the light expanded to fill the room.

Everything in his stomach tried to force its way back up his throat, but he swallowed it down. His intestines felt like they had emptied into his suit, and pressure on his eardrums forced him to squeeze his eyes shut. A hammer pounded against the inside of his skull. Blood trickled out of the corner of his mouth where he had bitten the inside of his cheek. The ground shifted under him, and before he could regain his balance, he toppled over and took the landing hard against his hip.

He opened his eyes, feeling sluggish, as if he had just awoken from a long nap. But he quickly snapped his head around, looking for whatever had been coming through the wormhole. Rolling to his feet, he saw a suited figure a few meters from him climbing to its feet. It wore a suit similar to his own D-Vac equipment, with motors at the joints and heavy plating overlapping each other like scales. Carter vaguely heard voices coming over the comm, but he ignored them as he brought his weapon to his shoulder and fired a blast of concentrated electrons. The pulse caught the alien in its chest plate and bore straight through it, shorting out a power pack it carried on its back and engulfing it briefly in flames before it exploded into pieces.

He shook his head, trying to clear it. The persistent voices in his earpiece pulled his attention back to the situation. A quick glance around revealed the forms of all five sailors and four marines. Everyone appeared no worse for wear and either climbed to their feet or were already up and ready in the case of the marines.

"Sound off," he shouted into his mic.

Skeeter and Guzman answered right away, along with the marines. He was about to call out again, when Wilson grunted.

"Ensign?" Carter asked.

"Here, Chief," Rae responded finally.

The ensign was the last to gain his feet, and when he looked up at the chief, his eyes widened and his gasps were audible over the comm-link. "What did you do, Chief?"

Chief Carter shrugged and looked around. The chamber beneath the surface of the moon had been replaced by a stone platform beneath a sun that radiated light as bright and intense as on a desert noon day. "May have been some sort of backlash. Matter trying to travel both ways, or something like that, must have caused the field to grow and brought us here through some sort of Einstein-Rosen Bridge."

"And where is here, Chief?" Ensign Rae snarled.

A long valley opened up below them, surrounded by gray, ragged rocks that crowned the ridges around them. Trees with bluish, narrow leaves on branches reaching to the ground like ankle-length grass skirts covered the mountainsides and the valley floor.

"Who joined our little party?" he asked the marines.

One of the four looked around at the others and then stepped forward. Pointing to the others around him one at a time, he answered,"PFC Martin, Corporal Hart, and Lance Corporal Strickland. I'm Gunnery Sergeant Warrow, but you can just call me Red, Chief."

"Will do, Red," Carter said."Thanks for tagging along." He looked around at their surroundings."Let's try to find out what we're going to do before we run out of air."

The stone area they had appeared on had been carved with similar designs as the one they had found in the chamber, and stood in a clearing perhaps fifty meters across. Chief Carter didn't have time to see if the patterns matched the ones back on the moon, because his HUD flashed movement in the sky down the valley. His visor focused on three flying vehicles heading up the valley at high speeds.

"Incoming, Chief," Skeeter warned him.

"Got them." He looked around the clearing."Any sign of a welcoming party?"

"Besides the three coming up the valley?" Wilson asked.

"Yeah, sailor."

Wilson grunted in the mic."Looks like the energy surge smoked anything that had been here waiting for us." He motioned with the end of his rifle towards what looked like a large stone lectern a couple meters away from the patterned stone. Lying beneath it was the charred and smoking husk of something that had been roasted to nothing more than a pile of ash.

"Then we need to fall back to that tree line and get out of sight," Chief Carter said."We don't know what level of technology they possess."

"Really, Chief?" asked Skeeter."We've just been flicked who-knows-where in the universe by a pillar of blue light, and we're wondering if they have advanced technologies?"

Carter tapped the side of his helmet and answered,"Point taken, Skeeter. Drop the smartass attitude and hustle to that tree line. It doesn't mean anything anyway until we recon. Now, move it!"

Chief Carter led them to a stand of trees twenty meters from the energy platform on the opposite side of the control panel. Not unlike trees on Earth, they stood fifteen meters tall but had branches covered with thick greenish-blue foliage from ground level all the way to the top. They crashed into the woods, and he imagined that if they hadn't been wearing the suits, that it would have felt like they had barged into a thicket of wire bushes. A low ridge drifted down to the right, and Chief Carter motioned everyone down behind it after the marines took up position at its top.

They had just settled out of sight in the woods when Carter felt a pressure against him, as if he were standing waist-deep in the surf off Coronado Island. Ripples shimmered like summer heat off a highway through the air above it. The three vehicles circled the plateau once before hovering over the clearing. Rather than being powered by flame and combustion as most Earth vehicles, the alien ships appeared to operate on concentrated pulses of air that sent out the disturbances that he felt. An unseen engine or power source sucked the air in through an intake located on the sides of the vessels and it pushed it out in alternating rhythms from exhaust portals both at the rear and underside of the vehicles. Chief Carter noticed the design allowed them to land vertically as two of the ships settled to the ground at the edge of the stone platform, while the third hovered for a few more seconds in a cover pattern before landing.

Putting his hand on Skeeter's shoulder, Chief Carter held up five fingers and then pointed to the side of his helmet. He chinned his comm unit to channel five and waited for Skeeter to give him the thumbs up.

"I hope they don't have access to the same frequencies we have," he said,"but we have to take the risk."

Skeeter just nodded, and motioned to Guzman to turn to the correct channel. While she passed the command on, Carter looked up at the top of the ridge where the four marines all had their weapons aimed and ready at the platform.

Chief Carter said to the marines,"Make sure your suit cams are on. If they operate those controls, I want to be able to duplicate it so we can get home."

"Got it, Chief," Red answered.

He looked over at Skeeter."I need you to transmit your recordings of the platform back on the moon to the ensign."

"Aye-aye, Chief." Skeeter pulled a cable from his suit forearm and handed it to Ensign Rae."Plug me in, sir. We'll get this uploaded into your system."

"Red?" Carter called.

"Yes, Chief?"

"Can you shortwave what your cams are picking up to the ensign?"

"Not a problem."

Ensign Rae turned his head to look at Carter."What are you planning, Chief? If we are going to start any confrontation, I will need to lead."

Carter flattened his right hand and swept it across his body in front of him."Negative, sir. If we can capture the sequence on the control panel, we need you to analyze it and get us out of here."

The only thing Chief Carter heard was the hum of his open comm channel because the ensign just sat there blinking. After a few uncomfortable moments, the ensign tapped the side of his helmet.

"We've got action up here, Chief," Red said.

Hugging close to the ground, Carter made his way up until he could see over the ridge. Two suited figures already stood by what he took for to be the control panel, their arms waving about. They pushed aside the pile of charred debris and returned to the panel where they started running their hands over it.

Sparks of blue light started to run through the patterns on the platform, gathering in the center before jumping up to coalesce into a spinning ball of energy, just like the one back beneath the surface of the moon. Seconds later, it flashed into a broad wall of light.

"If this is an invasion, Chief," Red began,"then how come there are only three ships?"

Chief Carter turned his hand top to bottom and back."I was just thinking that. It is probably just a scouting mission. I don't think they realized that we would have been digging beneath the surface."

Red rapped his helmet."That's the way I'd do it, Chief. A little recon never hurts." He pointed to the three ships."But if those are carrying troops and they go through the wormhole, or whatever it is, they could catch a lot of people by surprise and wreak some havoc before we have time to warn them."

"I agree," Carter replied."Let's hope we can get back."

He turned around and slid back down the slope."Can you get us back, sir?"

Rae tapped the panel on this forearm, watching as the two aliens in front of the controls waved their hands through colored beams of light that came up twenty centimeters off the surface of the panel.

"I believe so, Chief," he answered.

"Good," Chief Carter said."When we go over this ridge, it will be fast and hard. I want the marines on either flank in a pincer move with Guzman, Wilson, and me bearing hard down the middle. Ensign Rae and Skeeter will bring up the rear behind us. When I give the command, everyone launch their frags between them and the wormhole in a spread from left to right."

"I don't think that's a good idea, Chief," the ensign said."As ranking officer, I think we need to discuss what would be the best possible scenario. What do you think, Gunnery Sergeant Warrow?"

Red motioned across this chest with his flat hand."Negative, sir. Chief has the best plan."

"Why would you say that, marine?" Rae asked, his voice rising in pitch.

"Because of that, sir." Red pointed to the SEALS trident etched into Chief Carter's chest plate."I'd rather follow a SEALS into combat than an engineer, sir. Not meaning any disrespect, but Sea, Air, Land and Space gets my vote any day of the week."

After grunting once, Ensign Rae waved his hand in a dismissive gesture and waited for the others to move into position. Strickland and PFC Martin nodded at Red and moved down the ridge to Carter's right. The gunnery sergeant and Private Hart moved to the left, setting up and carefully watching the platform.

Chief Carter peered over the top of the ridge and watched the two figures in front of the control panel as they walked back and forth. They motioned towards some of the debris they had left after Carter had shot the first alien. Broad doors on the ends of each of the three vehicles swung down and hit the ground, stirring up pieces of dirt and clouds of dust. Twenty figures in armored suits trotted out of each ship and moved towards the portal. The first few moved up to the wall of light and stepped through without hesitating. They simply walked into the energy wave and disappeared.

Chief Carter looked to the right side of their line."When we go, I want Strickland to put two quick shots through the two at the panel. We can't let them shut it down."

"I can get us back," Ensign Rae said.

"I know, sir," Carter said."But I'd rather not have to worry about it."

When he looked back towards the platform, the entire group from the first ship had already gone through the wormhole, and half the second squad had disappeared as well.

"Now!" he shouted.

They exploded up over the ridge and through the wiry foliage at the edge of the clearing. He couldn't hear it, but Chief Carter saw the two aliens at the control panel take compressed energy bolts through their helmets before they crumpled to the ground. The far side of the platform erupted in gouts of fire and shrapnel when the frags exploded. Firing his own pulse rifle, he caught three of the aliens in the back before they realized the direction of the attack. Beside him, Guzman fired her rifle several times and dropped at least two more of the armored aliens.

One of them turned and fired its weapon from the hip. The bolt streaked across the clearing and hit Guzman in the right thigh. She grunted over the open comm, and Chief Carter heard her gasp and quickly suck in air through gritted teeth. He glanced at her but knew the D-Vac suit would release liquid carbon over the suit breach, creating a temporary seal to protect her against both the vacuum back on the moon and whatever microorganisms floated around in the alien atmosphere.

Chief Carter put a shot of compressed energy through one of the aliens that had turned around to face them, and he noticed that the rest of the second group had already gone through the wormhole. He swallowed a quick laugh when he realized that he and the others were actually the aliens here. One of the armored figures fired at the two marines on Carter's right, and he heard one of them grunt in pain as a bolt slammed through the chest plate of his suit. The marine went to one knee but fired at two more before toppling to the ground.

"We lost Martin," Strickland said over the comm.

"I saw," replied Red."And he took two of those assholes with him. Tighten up and sweep left. Let's meet in the middle."

The marines turned up the barrage of energy pulses, with Carter adding his own quick and accurate strikes. It wasn't long before they reached the edge of the stone dais. Breathing hard, Chief Carter stepped onto the platform and shot the remaining alien just as it turned and attempted to escape through the wormhole. He looked around and saw the ground littered with over twenty of the armored figures. Other than Martin, all the others joined him on the platform. A quick glance at the display panel on the inside forearm of his suit told him that the attack had lasted less than fifteen seconds.

"Do you have any explosives, Gunny?" Carter asked. He pointed over to the control panel as he trotted back with Strickland to retrieve Martin."We need to destroy that so no one follows us through."

Red patted the right thigh of his suit and opened a little compartment."Wouldn't leave home without 'em."

"Belay that order, Gunnery Sergeant," Ensign Rae said. He walked over to the control panel, avoiding the two corpses, and looked down at its surface."This is important technology that the United States government could use."

"Disregard, Red," Carter said. He raised his right hand when Ensign Rae whirled around, his face growing red through the visor."I understand what you want to do, sir. But if we leave this open, we're just inviting them to send reinforcements through behind us."

Ensign Rae frowned before he returned,"The risk is worth it, Chief."

Carter slid his flattened hand across the air in front of him."Sir, we have all this recorded. We have everything we need for the scientists and physicists back on Earth to reverse engineer it," he pointed out.

"Okay," said Ensign Rae after a second of silence."Carry on."

Red pulled out a pack of high-intensity explosives and knelt down. He opened the pack and spread the strip out over the top of the panel, unrolling it like a roll of paper towels. While he set the charges, Hart and Skeeter stood by the wormhole and kept their eyes and weapons focused down the valley.

Strickland shouldered Martin's pulse rifle and then grabbed the marine's legs. Chief Carter bent over and put his hands under Martin's arms. Together they carried him back to the platform and set him down in front of the shimmering wall of energy.

"We've got two minutes," Red said as he came up to the wormhole."We do not need to be here when this goes off."

Ensign Rae held his hands up."Wait. How do we know that destroying the panel here won't collapse the wormhole while we're in transit?"

Carter turned his right hand palm up and back."We don't. But I believe travel through a wormhole is instantaneous. My biggest worry is that the blast will come through after us. But I think that's unlikely, since the panel is almost twenty meters from the wormhole. Once the controls are destroyed, I'm betting that the singularity will collapse."

"I thought you weren't a physicist, Chief," Rae said, and Carter could hear the sneer in his voice.

"On-the-job training, sir," Carter replied. He motioned towards the flickering wall of energy in front of them."Let's get going instead of pissing in the wind."

Red and Strickland picked Martin's body up between them, holding their rifles ready in their free hands. Chief Carter pointed for Hart to go through first with Skeeter beside him. Wilson stepped in beside him, while Ensign Rae let Guzman lean on his shoulder at the rear behind Red and Strickland as they carried Martin's body.

Carter watched as Hart and Skeeter stepped into the wormhole. The air around them flickered briefly, and then they faded away to single points of light like an old television tube being turned off. He and Wilson followed.

As soon as they stepped into the curtain of energy, Chief Carter recalled a program he once watched that said travel through a wormhole would be instantaneous as it sidestepped time and space. To him it felt like the eternity of a dream-filled sleep – no time at all seemed to pass from the moment he shut his eyes and the moment he opened them, but he could remember the events that took place with vivid clarity as if he had lived a lifetime.

His skin tingled like his tongue would when he touched a 9-volt battery to it in his youth. Waves of cold and warmth washed through him so he didn't know whether to shiver or sweat. A featureless gray tunnel narrowed his vision for that brief moment he stepped through the singularity. He blinked and then stepped out of the energy into a scene of pure chaos.

His heart started racing and adrenaline coursed through his veins, driving out any remnants of chill. The first thing he saw was Skeeter dragging Hart over to the side of the room. They had returned to the chamber beneath the surface of the moon. Directly in front of him, over twenty armored aliens were caught in a fight to get out of the stone cavity into the tunnels. Chief Carter could hear chatter over the comm channels the moment he stepped out of the wormhole. Though he couldn't hear it, his HUD revealed that the aliens had encountered an armed platoon of marines when they had entered into the tunnels.

Chief Carter pinged the defenders to let them know they were friendlies and lifted his rifle, shooting the alien heading towards Skeeter and the injured Hart. The alien fell, dust puffing up around his form when it hit the ground. Beside him, Wilson ran low towards Skeeter, firing back at the entrance without looking. Together, they started pulling Hart behind some debris. Carter skipped towards the rear of the aliens, firing as he went. Red and Strickland joined him as soon as they stepped through the wormhole.

The three attacked the rear of the alien force, catching them by surprise and pinching them into a crossfire between themselves and the defending unit of marines. Carter patted Red on the shoulder when his rifle was out of energy and rolled behind a boulder to reload. After he shoved the new energy pack into his weapon, he stepped back into the fray. He heard Wilson cry out in pain. When he looked back, he saw that the left side of Wilson's D-Vac suit had a gaping hole, but the liquid carbon had already covered it and had started hardening. Behind Wilson, the wall of energy blinked out of existence as if it had never been there to start with.

The fight was quick but fierce. When Red called the all-clear, Carter could see other marines moving down the tunnel towards him with their rifles held out cautiously in front of them. Chief

Carter pinged the approaching squad and received an answering chime a second later.

"This is Captain Adam Holyfield," a gruff voice barked in his ear."Who are you?"

Chief Carter tried to swallow but realized that he hadn't taken a sip of water since they had first encountered the shimmering ball of energy."HTC Chief Carter. Crew leader of excavation crew Echo 6-Victor." He paused and looked to his side where Red waited."And this is Gunnery Sergeant Red Warrow, sir."

"Glad to see you guys made it out, Chief," Captain Holyfield said.

The marines stopped in front of Carter and Red but didn't lower their rifles. Chief Carter waved his hand behind him."We have wounded, sir. Can we get them topside?"

A marine in combat D-Vac armor stepped out of the group. Gold captain bars were etched into his chest panel."Of course, Chief."

Ensign Rae helped Guzman down the hall from the chamber past the marine captain. Behind him, Skeeter and Wilson had an arm under Hart's shoulders as the three dragged themselves down the tunnel.

Red and Strickland returned to the wormhole chamber to retrieve Martin's corpse while Carter gave Captain Holyfield a shortened version of the events that had led them to another planet and back. The marine listened silently as Carter revealed their adventure and their decision to return in hopes to warn the lunar base.

Captain Holyfield contacted the base nearly a kilometer above their heads. Ensign Rae and Strickland, along with Skeeter and Wilson, helped take the wounded and dead topside. Holyfield had lost four from his squad, and another three had severe enough wounds that they were evacuated as quickly as possible. Red and Carter stayed in the tunnels for nearly an hour, helping to set up blockades and electronic surveillance drones in the wormhole chamber. The remaining marines barraged them both with questions, but Chief Carter suggested to the captain that they keep everything close to the chest until Naval Intelligence and the Commanding Officer had a chance to debrief them. After power had been lost to the elevator, base command had sent Captain

Holyfield and his marines down to find out why no one was answering all the hails.

Every joint and muscle in his body ached with sudden fatigue the moment Carter stepped into the lift and it began its ascent up into the base. He and Red enjoyed the ride in silence, each alone in their thoughts.

Four military police burst into the carriage as soon as the lift doors opened, grabbing Chief Carter by the arms and informing him that he was under arrest. He looked over at Red and saw the marine frowning behind his faceplate. Carter turned his palm up and down and walked with the MPs down the halls to the small brig. They allowed him to cycle out of his suit and freshen up in a shower before assigning him to an isolated cell. He watched silently as two NCIS investigators came in and grabbed his suit, leaving without saying a word or even looking in his direction.

Though he remained silent, his mind raced through all the different scenarios that could have happened or that did happen as he rested on the narrow cot and stared up at the ceiling. Obviously, Ensign Rae had followed through with his threat to have him court-martialed for insubordination. The fact that the sniveling little rodent would rather play politics and protect his own ass than realizing that together they had all insured the safety of the moonbase and possibly the entire human race sickened him.

He figured he had been there a couple of hours when he heard the voices of Skeeter and Wilson down the hall. The two sailors were soon standing outside his cell, their mouths peeled back in wide grins.

"It's going to be even longer before you make senior chief now," Skeeter joked.

He looked over at Wilson, who added, nodding,"Yep. Hell, they might even drop you back to first class."

The two men laughed, and Chief Carter couldn't help but smile."Probably. It's happened before." He put his legs over the side of the cot and sat up."What's going on? Have you heard anything?"

Skeeter shrugged."Not much. The ensign has been behind closed doors with the big brass all day."

"They commandeered all our suits and the footage we shot," Wilson added.

"What do you think will happen, Chief?" Skeeter asked.

Carter wrinkled his nose."I don't know. Probably a hearing to see if I will stand before a court-martial." He scraped his bottom teeth over his top lip, and then sucked in a quick breath."How's Guzman?"

Wilson grinned."She's going to be all right. She's just as worried about you as we are. Plus, the corpsmen are having a hard time getting her to stay in the hospital."

"I can imagine," Carter grunted."Good for her."

The two sailors exchanged looks, and the smiles faded from their faces."They only gave us a few minutes, Chief," Skeeter said."But we'll come back and see you."

"Thanks, guys."

"That is, if they don't ship you back to Earth or vent you out an airlock," Wilson added, grinning.

After the two men left, he lay back down and tried to nap. He only managed a couple of hours' sleep before two military police opened his cell and put him in restraints. Carter took comfort that they cuffed him with his hands in front rather than having his arms bent at an uncomfortable angle behind his back. They led him down the halls to Admiral David Watters' office, Commanding Officer of USNA Moonbase Lunar One. A couple quick raps on the door elicited instructions to come in.

When he entered the room, Carter saw Admiral Watters behind an ornate desk of cherry wood, lit with a brass lamp. Two manila folders lay on the top to his left, and six books on the history of various Western conflicts stood between two bookends – one an anchor and the other a globe – at the right corner. A plain wooden frame rested on the top left corner, but Carter could not see the picture.

Two other officers sat on either side of the Admiral between the desk and the shelves behind them that covered the wall and that were lined with rows of books, obscure historical titles, and treatises on leadership and military operations. The officer on the Admiral's left was Captain Frank Ladd, the base executive officer, and the other was Commander Kurt Bisel, head of the NCIS division on the base. Ensign Rae stood at one side of the desk, moved far enough away that he wasn't blocking Captain Ladd's view of Chief Carter as he came into the room.

Admiral Watters motioned for the MPs to remove the handcuffs. As soon as his hands were free, Chief Carter snapped to attention and saluted the admiral and the other two senior officers. The admiral returned the salute while the other two officers were studying datapads in front of them. Ensign Rae never moved, but remained standing casually to the side, silent and watching. Chief Carter glanced over at Rae and thought he detected a slight sneer from the corner of the ensign's mouth.

Chief Carter remained standing, silently. He saw Ladd and Bisel thumb through their datapads, occasionally writing notes, and the Admiral looked back and forth between the two.

"First off, Chief Carter," Captain Ladd said, and looked up,"I want to commend you on a job well done. If you hadn't acted with assertiveness and foresight, we very well could not have had the opportunity to be here today."

From the corner of his eyes, Chief Carter saw the ensign's brows furrow into a deep frown."Be that as it may," Captain Ladd continued,"Ensign Rae reports that you willfully disregarded several orders that he issued to you over the course of your little adventure to parts unknown."

Carter didn't respond and waited for the XO to continue, but it was Commander Bisel that spoke up."We have taken the liberty of looking up your service record, Chief Carter."

"Yes, sir," Carter said."That would be prudent."

Bisel nodded."It is littered with not only commendations, but it appears that you sometimes have a problem with authority. Is that an accurate assessment, Chief?"

"If that is how it read, Commander, then I will not contest anything that is written in it."

Admiral Watters nodded, and held up his hand to keep Commander Bisel from continuing."I have a couple of questions for you, Chief."

"Yes, sir."

Looking down at his own datapad, Admiral Watters asked,"Is it accurate that you called Ensign Rae a damn fool?"

Chief Carter shook his head."Not exactly, sir."

"We don't have time for a dance with semantics, Chief," the admiral said, shaking his head."What exactly did you call him?"

Still standing at attention, Carter replied,"I said that in my opinion, he was a damn fool, sir."

Admiral Watters nodded."You have played this game before, I see, Chief."

"Yes, sir."

Commander Bisel chuckled while the other two senior officers made no attempt to hide their smiles. Carter clenched his jaw tightly, preventing him from breaking out in a grin of his own.

Ensign Rae spoke up, his voice timid and quiet."Admiral Watters. If I may ask a question?" The Admiral nodded once, and Rae continued,"I fail to understand why this enlisted man is not being reprimanded for his intentional disobeying of a direct order and for his disrespectful conduct towards a superior officer."

Captain Ladd looked over at Admiral Watters."May I answer this one, Admiral?" Watters nodded, and Captain Ladd glared at the ensign, his face muscles tightening and the left corner of his mouth twitching."Listen here, Ensign Rae. You would be dead right now if Chief Carter had listened to your orders. And you obviously weren't paying attention at the Academy the day they taught ethics."

Darting looks back and forth between Carter and Captain Ladd, Ensign Rae's brows furrowed to a narrow point above the bridge of his nose and he licked his lips three times."Even an enlisted man is allowed an opinion," Ladd continued."But one with the service record of Chief Carter has a valued opinion."

"But he disobeyed a direct order, sir," the ensign protested, his voice pitching up in a whine.

"I agree," said Captain Ladd."And it will be reflected in his service jacket."

"Is that it?" Rae asked.

"Should there be more?" the captain responded.

"I…I thought…" Ensign Rae stammered, but he couldn't finish his sentence and stood there with his mouth gaping.

Admiral Watters spoke up,"Ensign Rae?"

"Yes, sir?"

"Is it true that you have a degree in structural engineering?"

"Yes, sir," Rae replied, puffing out his chest.

"Is it true that you have been accepted to Stanford University to study Advanced Astro-engineering this fall?"

"Yes, sir," Ensign Rae snapped, standing straighter and pulling his shoulders back.

Admiral Watters grimaced."I'm afraid you will no longer be carrying out that assignment."

Ensign Rae's eyes widened, and his lip quivered."What?"

"Is that the way you are to address your commanding officer, Ensign?" Captain Ladd barked at the young man.

"I'm sorry, sir." Ensign Rae shuddered and lowered his head."I respectfully request to ask the admiral the reason he has said what he just did."

Captain Ladd turned to Watters, who nodded."Easy, Ensign Rae," said the captain after he turned back."You will face a summary court-martial as your actions directly led to the needless death of two servicemen. You failed to listen to the advice of skilled and experienced sailors when just listening would have prevented any loss of life. Because of your incompetence, Lunar One and subsequently the Earth were almost successfully invaded by a hostile species."

After Captain Ladd finished and sat back in his chair, Admiral Watters pointed an aged finger at the ensign."I assure you, Ensign Rae, it will be a privilege to see you drummed out of the service for your idiocy. You do not deserve to wear that uniform."

Ensign Rae opened and shut his mouth several times, but nothing came out. His eyes squinted as he looked at Captain Ladd, and he sniffed several times.

"You are dismissed, Ensign Rae," the Captain said.

Coming to attention, Rae saluted the officers, but no one returned it. He turned and walked towards the door, leering at Chief Carter as he passed."I bet this makes you happy. You're still just an enlisted man, Chief, while I have a degree and will be employed by top firms."

Carter remained at attention and didn't respond. He kept his eyes forward, looking at the admiral's bookshelves behind the desk.

"MPs!" Commander Bisel shouted. When the two MPs that had brought Chief Carter entered the room, he said,"Please, escort Ensign Rae to his quarters." The ensign continued to glare at Chief Carter."And if he sees fit to open his mouth at all during the journey," Bisel continued,"please, shut it for him."

The ensign turned to look at Bisel, who only smiled and

said,"Your degree didn't help you today, did it?"

When the ensign opened his mouth to speak, one of the MPs quickly smacked him in the back of his head."Let's go, Ensign. We have our orders," he said as they escorted him out of the office.

After a few silent seconds, the admiral looked up at Carter."Great job, today, Chief. I wish we had more people like you."

"Thank you, sir."

"You will be awarded the Navy Cross for this, Chief. You saved the world with your quick actions."

Captain Ladd added,"And not to mention the valuable research that was gathered because you had the foresight to record what you saw."

Chief Carter nodded,"Thank you, sirs. I just did my duty."

Commander Bisel shook his head,"No, Chief. You went way beyond. A grateful Navy and Earth thank you."

Carter opened his mouth to say something, but then thought better of it and closed it. He just nodded.

"What is it, Chief?" the Admiral asked."Did you want to add something?"

"Yes, sir," Chief Carter said, standing even straighter.

"Spit it out. You've earned the right."

Carter nodded."It's just that…" He paused, licking his lips and gripping the hemline of his pants with his right hand."I was wondering what we are doing for Petty Officer Second-Class Weasley, sir. Weezer had a wife and two young kids."

The admiral nodded."Always concerned about your men, Chief. That's what makes you so valuable to this Navy."

He pulled one of the two folders on his desk over in front of him and opened it."Petty Officer Weasley will be getting the Purple Heart and a Bronze Star. His wife will be taken care of for the rest of her life. This isn't the 21st century, Chief. We take care of our own."

"Yes, sir," Chief Carter said. He saluted, which all three officers answered smartly. He turned on his heel and walked out of the room, allowing a smile to cross his face for the first time since the MPs took him from his cell.

LUNAR RUSE

By
Paul Kevin Findley

"Zach!"

"Ow!" Zachary Claveaud rose from the hospital bed niche too quickly and banged his head on the low ceiling."I'm going to have a concussion if you keep surprising me, Gwen." He began rubbing his scalp.

Habitat One's Station Commander, Gwen Patrick, looked at him with amusement."Take an aspirin and come with me. Bed rest is over; it looks like you get to wear your second hat this month after all."

Claveaud's primary duties as a civil engineer were to reinforce and expand the lava tubes first discovered by the Kaguya spacecraft in 2009 that served as platforms for the moon base's living quarters and research facilities. His "second hat" was that of Marshal for Habitat One. Since it was a joint US/Japan effort, the engineer and former Air Force officer trained at the Marshal's Academy in Glynco, Georgia and the Criminal Investigation Bureau in Tokyo.

"If it's Frick and Frack stealing each other's brewing supplies again, I feel too poorly to leave sickbay yet. Cough! Cough!" The Louisiana native groaned and tried to lie back on the bunk.

"Nice try, Zach; Dr. Evans already told me your lungs are

clear. Now get up, there's a body for you to examine."

He rolled out smoothly, missing the ceiling and landing softly on his feet. Patrick handed him a camera package the doctor had asked for and led him out into the corridor.

"Who is it?" Both began leaping their way to the main entrance rather than using the micro-tacky paths needed to walk normally under lunar gravity.

"Ted Donaldson."

"Where's the body?"

"West Crater, about 400 meters from Neil Armstrong's footprints. Evans is waiting for you."

***

Claveaud drove parallel to the tracks leading to West Crater and parked 20 meters from the edge. Habitat One's doctor, Bartholomew Evans, was waving at him.

"*Bon après-midi*, Doctor." Claveaud leaped carefully down the crater, keeping parallel to the existing footprints.

"Good afternoon to you too, Zachary."

"Here's your camera kit. Have you moved the body or anything around it?"

"No. I'm going to record the position of the body and examine his eyes and skin through the helmet before we move him inside. I'll download the report to you once I'm finished." Evans attached the two cameras to his suit and began recording.

"Gwen said Paul found the body. Where is he?" Paul Nordling was the Chief of Suit Maintenance and Habitat One's historian.

"He'll be back in a few minutes with a crawler."

Claveaud shook his head inside the helmet."He should have remained until I arrived."

"Paul was out testing a new type of knee joint when he saw Ted at 13:53. He was running low on oxygen, so he went for a new airpack after he called me. I was nearby on my monthly check walk, so I arrived quickly and then called Commander Patrick."

"How long was the body unattended?"

"Less than four minutes."

Claveaud looked around for fresh tracks, but only saw the one path down to Ted's body and his own tracks.

"There go my recent footprints."

"Oh! I'm sorry, Zachary. I didn't think about that."

"It's OK, Doc. Paul did the same thing. Go ahead and finish your initial report; I'll examine the immediate area and try not to interrupt you again." He blinked twice at the comm icon on his helmet's heads-up display and waited.

"Zach, have you found anything yet?"

"It's what I haven't found that bothers me, Gwen. I'm going to need a list of suit and rover GPS locations going back one hour and moving forward to now, 14:33." He began establishing a perimeter, placing warning beacons as he spoke."Anything within 100 meters of Ted's body at that time should have seen him or at least realized he was out here."

Technically, there was no Global Positioning System on the moon. It rotated only once every 28 days, requiring the satellites to be so high over the surface that they would be affected by Earth's gravity as well. To keep satellites low enough to be useful, they were constantly adjusting acceleration.

"I'm not a research assistant or one of your part-time deputies Zach."

Claveaud could almost see her mouth twist into a wry smile."I'll call Frick myself, Gwen. I just wanted to let you know before I did so."

"Neither Wetzel nor York appreciate your nicknames for them."

"With both of them named Frederick, it's too easy. Besides, I got sick of the argument about German Lagers versus English Ales about three months ago. It's all beer and that's what counts when the bartender puts the glass in your hand."

"What about the video feed?" Gwen asked. In an effort to help the Habitat One residents stay a little saner, NASA and JAXA set up cameras over the work areas, historic sites and key points such as the Eagle Landing and Earthrise. All were on a 24-hour feed to the Habitat and Earth.

"Ted's body is outside the camera range; I'm going to need the suit and rover locations to see if anyone was close to him when the accident happened. If it looks like someone did cross the Eagle feed, I can access it any time."

"You know it was an accident already?"

"It looks like it, but I won't sign my name to it just yet, Gwen. Go ahead and put the word out officially that there was an accident and to stay away from West Crater."

***

"OK, gentlemen; pick him up carefully. I'll grab his feet." Zach watched Evans and Nordling each grab a shoulder, and in a few minutes, they had the suit out of the crater and on the crawler.

"Paul, make sure to secure the body so it doesn't bounce."

"I got him, Zach." They quickly clipped the suit to tie-down points and Nordling double-checked everything.

"Doctor, did you get all the pictures you needed?"

"Yes, Zachary."

"Good. The two of you start back. When you get to the airlock, wait for me. I'm going to take one last look around."

As they left, Claveaud made sure his perimeter was secure and took one final video of the entire scene. Anyone who crossed the electronic crime scene tape would be recorded from multiple points at the same time an alarm was sent to Zach's comm. The marshal muttered to himself as he climbed into his rover.

"What were you doing out here, Ted? You were always too busy trying to build your own legacy to appreciate anyone else's." He engaged the battery and then turned the rover back to the Habitat. When he arrived at the airlock, the marshal found Evans and Nordling waiting for him with Ted on a skid.

Paul gestured inside."We have a crowd waiting for us, Zach."

"Great." Claveaud shook his head, then saw Commander Patrick along with everyone else."Looks like the boss is here to run interference for us. Let's get inside and get this started."

The three shed their suits as quickly as possible, but left Ted in his. Doctor Evans took over.

"We'll take him directly to Sickbay, suit and all. Doctor Yamamoto and the nurses have two exam tables linked together for us. Fortunately, you were my only patient, Zachary."

"What about your tools to crack open the suit, Paul?"

"My crew chief should already be there with them. The doc and I handled it on our private comm channels."

"Open the door, then."

To Claveaud's surprise, the crowd was quiet.

Gwen must have had time to calm them down. Let's see if I can work with that.

"I know everyone has questions. Right now, I don't have any answers. Once we have a full autopsy and a complete suit check, I'll have something for you."

"OK, everyone!" Gwen jumped in with her best command voice."Let them get to Sickbay!"

***

Once everything was photographed and catalogued for evidence, Paul took the suit to his workshop to begin a complete examination. Evans began his autopsy, and Claveaud went to the Communications Office to consult with Frederick Wetzel about the suit and rover locations. Frick was one of Claveaud's deputies if he needed him.

"I have one vehicle and one suit that were within the timeframe you wanted, Zachary."

"What are the designations, and where are they now?"

"The rover is A-4; common use. It's parked in its charging station. According to the log, Ted checked it out at 0914."

"That figures." Claveaud grimaced."Whose suit is it?"

"The suit is HM-5, common worker."

"Who used it?"

"The log was bypassed, but it was disconnected from its charging station at 0843. It's not powered up, so let's turn on its beacon and ...well, that's odd. It doesn't show up." Wetzel started his remote diagnostics."It appears that someone not only pulled the battery out of HM-5, they also deactivated the beacon."

"Isn't that supposed to be impossible?" Claveaud leaned closer to the screen.

"According to Paul Nordling and NASA, it should be." Wetzel nodded in agreement."Whoever did this actually had to cut the beacon out, but that still doesn't completely hide the suit. Even when damaged or if the power source is unplugged or impaired, the beacon sends out an emergency signal that provides the last location, which didn't happen in this case." The comm chief leaned back in his seat and began rubbing his neck."If you drop it down a

35

deep enough hole, say 100 meters at least, or bury it under a landslide on the dark side, you could block the signal. We haven't placed any satellites over the DS to enhance the signal, either. No one goes over there yet, Zach."

"There isn't a hole that deep in the habitat, Frederick; but there are a couple nearby. What about using a signal booster on those to try and find it?"

"Perhaps. If you think it will help, Zach, I'll run some models with Geography and Mapping to figure out the best places to search over on the DS as well."

"Thanks, Frederick. Let me know if Hiroko and her team find anything."

"Does this mean you'll stop with the 'Frick and Frack'?"

Zachary laughed."If you and York can stop stealing yeast and hops from each other for an entire month, I'll think about it."

The communications chief waved his hand dismissively."We're done with that. York and I decided to join efforts and construct the first commercial brewery on the moon. We're going to sell beer back to Earth."

"You really think Gwen will go for that?"

"We've worked up a good business plan, and with the novelty of everything related to the Habitat, we think that we'll more than cover all costs."

"*Chance* to the both of you, then."

***

Commander Patrick put her elbows on her desk and her chin in her hands.

"Does it still look like an accident, Zach?"

"Well, it appears that Ted took a misstep at the crater's edge. As he fell, he damaged his helmet and the coupling point between his suit and the airpack. Another bounce or two on his helmet and he would have cracked it wide open."

"So are you going to sign your name to it now?"

"Only as a preliminary report, Gwen. Until I find that missing suit and who was in it, I won't close this out. Someone has to explain why they didn't report the accident. Unless they shoved Ted off the edge and tried to cover it up."

"Did you get anything from the rover?"

Claveaud grimaced and shook his head."No, and with no cameras inside the Hab and the satellites unable to penetrate, I've got no way to track the suit before Wetzel activated the beacon. Do you want me to send out a mass v-mail explaining this to everyone?"

"No, Zach, I'll do it. I would like you to help me draft it, though. I'll attach it to my report back to JAXA and NASA. Word is already filtering back to Earth."

"Happy to oblige, Commander. Have you spoken with Tsutomu about a memorial service yet?" Tsutomu Okada was in charge of constructing and maintaining the base's solar panel arrays. He also served as the Habitat's chaplain and counselor.

"There won't be one. He said Ted's final wishes were very clear that he didn't want a formal ceremony. What Ted requested was an informal wake; anyone who wants to say something about him is welcome to get up and speak."

Zach rolled his eyes."*Qui est sans surprise.* Ted's set it up so everyone has to say how wonderful he was, risk alienation if they say otherwise, or just stay silent."

***

Paul Nordling called Claveaud early the next morning.

"You have something for me, Paul?"

"Yes, but it's not going to make your job easier. Get over here."

Claveaud quickly slipped on issue coveralls and station shoes. As he entered the Suit Maintenance Bay, Paul waved him over to the microscope display screen he was using."Do you see this cut on the coupling?"

"Is that the airpack connection for Ted's suit?"

The Chief of Suit Maintenance nodded."There are four others very similar to it. Not unusual, but when I isolate them from the other damage, you can see that all five are roughly equidistant. That's not accidental, Zach."

"No, that's sabotage; maybe even murder."

"Like I said, I'm not making your job any easier today."

Claveaud looked at the screen again and then back to Paul."I'll need a complete scan of the coupling and surrounding material from the suit and airpack so I can run it through my equipment. When that's completed, we'll put everything into an evidence locker. Then comes the hard part."

"This is easy?"

"Compared to telling Gwen she has a killer in the Hab? Yes." Claveaud cracked his neck and looked at the display again."One advantage to being in this situation: every tool and weapon we brought with us was scanned into my database before we lifted off."

***

"It's not in the database." Claveaud sat stunned for a moment, staring at his computer screen. Then he spilled every curse he knew in French and English and tried to figure out where the weapon could have come from. Paul had found traces of ceramic on the connection, so it could have been created using almost any 3D printer on the installation. Most of those belonged to Habitat One's quartermaster, Kevin Brown.

The marshal made sure Brown was in his office and then leaped down there as quickly as he could. Except for the 1,000 kilograms of personal property each team member brought onboard, everything used on Habitat One originated from Brown's inventory or came out of one of his printers.

Claveaud smiled to himself as he approached the quartermaster's offices. Gwen Patrick maintained a long tradition commanders had with quartermasters or inventory specialists. As a good boss, she made sure everyone had what they needed and then turned a benevolent, if suspicious, eye away from what happened after that.

"*Bonjour*, Kev!"

"Good morning, Marshal. What can I do for you today?" It was Brown's standard greeting to Claveaud since they first met at Johnson Space Center.

"Nothing for myself, Kevin. I just need a little information for my investigation, please."

"Anything to keep the wheels of justice turning, Marshal."

"Good." Claveaud set down his pad and activated the 3D

display of the edge that cut into Ted's airpack."This doesn't show up anywhere in my database. I need to find out where it was created."

Brown examined the display."If it's a short blade, it would have been made quickly. Are you certain it's not broken off a larger tool or weapon?"

Zachary shook his head no."The marks are too uniform for that. If it were a shard from a larger tool or weapon, there would have been indications of either a broken surface or a handle striking the coupling, airpack or suit."

"Is it safe to assume that this is smaller than the entrenching tool that comes with a rover's emergency kit?"

"Yes, that also would have left marks all over the airpack, suit and helmet."

Kevin scrolled through the notes on the pad."Between size and material, I can eliminate half of my printers right now."

"How so?"

"The larger machines won't print anything smaller than a cubic meter. Cost-saving restriction. Four of the smaller ones work with metal or plastic only. There's no way they could have printed this."

"How long will it take to run through the remaining printers?" Claveaud had at least one more interview for the day as well as a set of core samples to examine from the start of Tunnel Four.

"Not sure. I'll check first to see if any of the machines haven't printed anything with a cutting edge. That might eliminate another one or two, and then I'll check against the shape of the cut. It won't be tonight, but I'll have it for you by lunch tomorrow."

"Thanks, Kevin."

"Have you checked with Freddy York at Manufacturing?"

"He's next. Given the size I'm looking for, I figured you were the person to start with."

***

Claveaud had no better luck with Frederick York. With little privacy and fewer secrets at the station, he recommended to Commander Patrick to tell the department heads that evening what was going on before any rumors could take hold. She agreed and called a meeting that night in the main common area. After the marshal gave his report, Gwen laid out what was going to happen next.

"Since there's nowhere for you to go, a lockdown would be useless. From now on, all suits will be tracked. Paul Nordling has already activated the beacons, and they'll stay on until Marshal Claveaud finds out for certain what happened to Ted. Comms will also be set to auto-update movement between private quarters, common areas and work stations. I'm also asking each of you to set your personal pads to auto-update as well." The Habitat Commander blew out a breath and then asked what she didn't want to.

"Does anyone have a question?"

"How do we know he didn't do it?" The botany chief jumped up first."'Marshal Dillon' there hated Ted from the day we met at Johnson."

Claveaud smiled at Bonnie Essex-Nakamura."I was in sickbay for the 72 hours leading up to Ted's death coughing up concrete and regolith dust. Doc Evans had me monitored and under observation the whole time, Bonnie; just ask him."

"Humph!" Bonnie stared daggers at Claveaud but sat down.

Zachary continued."Look, whoever did this planned it well. As I said, they used a worker suit and somehow got a ride with Ted in the rover he checked out. Then they figured out how to override the safety alarm on Ted's suit and the emergency beacon on their own. By the time we started checking location data, it was too late to track the suit."

"Better late than never though, right?" the Chief of Geology and Seismology asked.

"Not in this case, Edwin. I should have had Wetzel activate the beacons in every suit the moment Gwen told me about finding Ted's body. Maybe I could have caught the killer on the bounce when he was returning to the station, or at least before he made the suit disappear."

"'Him'? You know it's a man?"

"Figure of speech, Hiroko."

The Chief of Geography and Mapping nodded her thanks.

Bonnie hotly called out,"That's sexist."

"If it'll make you feel better, I'll name you as a suspect and go tear your quarters apart right now." Claveaud continued to smile.

"Are you going to use this as an excuse to invade our privacy and ransack our homes?" The botany chief jumped to her feet again.

"Personal quarters will be searched, yes. Are you still trying to hide non-government grown cannabis in your bathroom, Bonnie?"

Essex-Nakamura muttered something under her breath and left quickly, almost bouncing into the ceiling. After Patrick informed the rest of the department heads there was nothing else, they left at an easier pace. Only Edwin Scott remained.

"It sounded like she called you a 'gashole,' Zachary."

"That's fine, Edwin. She and the other 'Screw Earth, let's build our own society' types are more scared than pissed off right now anyway. One of their own is dead and they're too concerned about me finding contraband than figuring out what happened. Then again, if one of them did it, that'll make my job easier."

"Can you really just tear up her quarters like that?"

"You signed the same agreement. Everyone who signed on for this mission gave up most of their personal rights as it relates to privacy or criminal investigation. Your intellectual property rights are rock solid, though. Any new tech or scientific theory you develop remains yours. Our governments can use it exclusively for one year if they want, but they have to pay very generous royalties even then."

"Ted was always crying about that." Edwin nodded in agreement."He kept pointing out Diego Martel from the Advance Team lost millions in that first year."

"Yeah, but he always left out that JAXA and NASA used their resources to help Martel refine his oxygen extractor and even helped him market it." Zachary laughed."Diego bought his own island after he returned to Earth and hasn't left it. If he needs anything, he has it flown in. He's not complaining. He's too busy counting how many countries whose annual GNP he out-earns every month."

The chief geologist grinned."Supposedly he has his own McDonald's making Shamrock Shakes year round." Edwin quickly became more serious."Picking up Ted's job along with mine is not going to make for a pleasant time, though."

"I think between you, Takeo and Akane Ito, it shouldn't take up all of your personal time."

"I know that, but tracking radiation coming in through the surface and monitoring the ground levels is a bit more life-and-death than I'm used to."

"The basic levels and standards have all been determined, Edwin."

"Which have to be checked against every foot of tunnel or living space you dig out."

"There are Geiger Counters on every machine. One rad over the recommended levels and it all shuts down automatically."

Scott refused to be comforted."Those have to be checked by me to make sure they work. I have everyone's life and reproductive futures in my hands."

Claveaud began shaking his head."*There's* an image I never want to think about again, Edwin."

***

The next morning, Claveaud met with the excavation crew to determine their new digging schedule before returning to his investigation.

"The Tunnel Four entrance is solid, Akane. We can push forward anytime you're ready to go."

Team Chief Ito nodded."I agree, Zach; how would you like Drill Two starting on Wednesday?"

"Sounds good. I should have the Tunnel Three refinish completed by then."

"Excellent! If there are no surprises with the initial digging, we're back on schedule to finish the tunnel system and start digging the family quarters."

Claveaud looked at Chief Ito sideways."Family Quarters are Hab Two's work. Are you really serious about staying here for the next phase?"

"Yes. Habitat Two is where we truly begin constructing our own city and not just building off of the lava tubes." Akane had spent most of his adult life in one mine or another all over Earth. There were few team members better suited for the claustrophobic life on the moon.

"After the partial collapse and now a suspicious death, I'm thinking I'm safer in New Orleans where I can at least breathe nonextracted air."

Akane nodded."You were lucky last week."

"No doubt, *mon ami*. If I'd inhaled a little more dust, I'd still be on bedrest. If I had been thirty feet closer, I'd be in a body cast."

The stocky excavator snorted."I thought you Cajuns were tough enough to sew your own severed leg back on and then run a marathon."

"Well, of course we are, but we're also smart enough that when someone tells us we have to be lazy, we'll stay in bed until they drag us out with a winch." Claveaud stretched and faked a yawn.

"Or if Gwen says there's a dead body?" Akane grinned at Zachary's sudden discomfort, but the marshal quickly waved off the hint.

"I merely responded to the call of duty."

"I do not believe that. Remember who covered for both of you when you snuck off-base. *Twice*."

"Was that you? I swear my memories of Earth are fading with every day that passes."

"You just don't want to admit Gwen got under your skin."

Zach grinned and switched into a heavy accent."There ain't no gettin' undah this gator hide, son! Why, my grand-pappy once had a bullet ric-o-chet right off his noggin'..."

"Get out, Zach!" Ito groaned, shaking his head and went back to his stress fracture reports. The only way to shut the civil engineer up when Zach dropped into a patois was to ignore him until he got tired of listening to himself or just throw him out.

***

"The autopsy report showed there were no chemicals in his blood or in the brain tissue sample. Everything appears normal, Gwen." Claveaud was back in Gwen's office to report what little he had discovered before the evening meal.

"Thank you, Zach." She looked at him for a moment, then continued."I've got a question for you. I know you're dedicated to the job, but you seem to be taking this personally. You and Donaldson had no love for each other, so why tear yourself up over it?"

The marshal gave a wry smile."Ted was a miserable excuse for a human being. After his affair with Samantha finished in that glorious crash and burn, he's lucky he didn't get locked outside the Hab. The only thing he ever did well was his job in getting us here and working with the engineering team to secure us all against catching too much radiation. I respected him for that. Whoever killed him and tried to cover it up showed him no respect at all, and I want to make sure they're punished for it."

"So this is only out of professional courtesy?" Gwen looked like she didn't believe him.

"Call it what you want. I'll do my job here, and you know it won't matter who gets their feelings hurt."

"Speaking of which, you're starting the Personal Quarters inspection today?"

"Yes, as soon as we're done here." Claveaud nodded and took a sip of the hot drink he had brought with him. Gwen twisted her nose in revulsion.

"I still don't see how you can drink that chicory." She changed the subject before Claveaud could respond."I guess Mike Eiling's now the leader of the 'Moon First' clique. What are you going to do if he makes a fuss?"

"I'll listen to his concerns, and if he has a point, I'll adjust accordingly." Claveaud broke into his best, innocent, little boy look."If Mike wants to cross the line like he did when we landed, I'll leave him with another limp."

Gwen smiled despite herself."You could have put him down that day without screwing up his knee like you did."

"Of course. But the low gravity helped him to heal faster, and let's face it, no one's tried to replace you since then." Zach brightened further."Hey, I just realized, replacing Ted as leader of their little group is sufficient motive for murder. I guess I'll start the quarters search this afternoon with him."

Gwen began rubbing her temples to ward off the coming headache."Please don't leave them a wreck, and when you do confront him, try not to break anything."

"Whatever you want, Commander Patrick." He left Gwen's office with a bow and a flourish.

***

Zachary placed a small case on the floor outside Eiling's quarters and opened it. The top and sides folded down, revealing a surveillance drone about the size of a large coffee mug with hover fans on either end.

"Activate." As the drone rose to eye level and switched on its recording devices, Claveaud gave it instructions."Maintain one camera on me, one on the room itself, and the third on all evidence I bag and carry out." He punched in his override code and then entered the room. The drone flew in with him and then maintained a distance appropriate so all three cameras captured everything possible.

"This is a Personal Quarters inspection related to the death of Theodore Simpson Donaldson. This unit is assigned to Michael Eiling, no middle name."

Single personal quarters were three meters high, three and a half meters wide, and five meters in length. Married or cohabitating personal quarters were three meters high, seven meters wide and eight meters in length.

Claveaud started with a"sniffer" to examine the air for any recent trace of surface moon dust. According to records, Mike hadn't been outside in three days and had gone through a complete decontamination. There should be a very low amount in the air content unless he had dropped a suit in a hurry and then walked away from it.

Once completed, he stripped the sheets and pillowcase from the bed and placed them in an evidence bag. Zachary set it on the floor, out of his way but still within view of the drone's cameras. He placed the pillow against the wall and scanned it with a handheld MRI device. After scanning a corner of the bed, he dropped the pillow on it and finished examining the air mattress. Finding nothing, he began removing books and smaller items from shelves and table surfaces.

Claveaud then began examining the larger items to include the furniture, disassembling some pieces and then reassembling them. He didn't particularly care if Eiling was inconvenienced, but he had promised Gwen, after all.

The bathroom was the last area examined. Zachary used the"sniffer" again to analyze the air in the separate room. With that done, he did the same examination with the bathroom items. Once completed, he gathered up the evidence bags and departed Eiling's quarters.

Claveaud left a note with a voice recording on the door, explaining what he had done and stated the appropriate regulations that covered his search. He ended it, letting the water maintenance chief know that he could request a copy of the search in person or by email after 0800 the next morning.

***

"Who the hell do you think you are, going into my quarters without my permission?"

Claveaud looked up from a set of sample results to see Eiling standing in his doorway."I think I'm the Marshal in Charge conducting an investigation of a suspicious death. As I said in the note, I had a drone recording everything; you can request the recording anytime you want to see it."

He turned his chair to face Mike, set down his chicory and continued."All of the items I took were base issue, nothing personal. I've already sent a list to Kevin Brown; you can pick up replacements right now if you want to."

"Screw that. You ever set foot in my quarters again without asking me and I'll break you in half."

"This is the only warning you'll get, Mike. If you want to try me again, you'll walk around with a cast and a cane this time."

The big engineer grinned."Won't be so easy this go-around. I've been working out with Takeo." He put his hands up and began moving quickly toward Claveaud."Come on, soldier boy!"

Zach placed a foot against the table and pushed off, neatly sidestepping Eiling. A hand pushed into the larger man's back forced him off-balance and slammed him into a wall. The water maintenance chief recovered, spun around and dropped into a formal *kata*.

"You call that a proper form, waterboy? C'mon over here!" He grinned as he said it, knowing Eiling hated the nickname. Mike charged him again, but Zach moved in quicker and caught the larger man midstride. The palm strike drove out his air and Mike stumbled backward, trying to breathe.

Claveaud slid in closer, wanting to stomp his opponent's ankle flat; but remembered Gwen Patrick's request. Instead, he kicked Eiling's feet out from under him and slapped the back of his head to speed Mike's way to the floor.

"Stay down."

The bigger man struggled to his feet."Suck a..."

Feeling his own temper starting to fray, Zach pulled his taser from his belt and fired. The needle nodes discharged 50K volts into Mike, dropping him to his knees and then laying him out flat.

"First off, I was an airman, not a soldier. Get it right or next time I'll thump you harder just to make a point." He returned the taser to its holster."In case you think I'm cheating *grand homme*, I'm not." He dragged Mike's twitching form into the single jail cell, removed the taser needles, stepped out and then secured the door."Commander Patrick asked me very politely not to bust you up again and my mama always taught me to grant a lady's wishes when it's within my ability to do so."

***

"I need him out and working, Zach." Gwen was unpleasantly surprised to find Claveaud back in her office so quickly. More so, after Zachary reported what happened.

"Attempted assault of station personnel does not require the person involved to even file charges, Commander. The minimum he can get away with is ten days."

"He claims you goaded him."

"The cameras were running from the moment he walked into my lab, Gwen. Unless he wants an extra day for swearing a false statement, you better tell him to shut his mouth."

"Regardless, I need him out. Nor can I afford to waste someone else's time watching him."

"My jail unit can be automated under isolation mode to include meal delivery up to three weeks. The only item a prisoner can damage is the toilet, and outside cameras will pick it up and ping me immediately if someone tries to jam it up with their clothing or bedding. If I do that, then I can let him out after five days." He checked the time display on Gwen's desk."Make that four and a half now."

"Mike and the rest of the 'Moon First' people are still arguing that falls under cruel and unusual punishment," she pointed out.

"They can argue all they want, but they agreed to it before we left Earth."

"Isn't there any 'law enforcement discretion' you can exert?"

"Yes, of course."

"Good! When can you let him out?"

Zach crossed his arms."Six days."

"Not funny, Marshal."

"You should have let me bust him up a little. Doc Evans could have overridden me with a medical release."

Gwen stiffened and switched to her station commander voice."Did you plan this when I asked you to restrain yourself, Marshal Claveaud?"

Claveaud realized immediately he had just crossed a line."No, Commander; I did not." He got up to leave."If you'll excuse me, I have interviews to conduct. Take the prisoner his dinner and then set the system to let him out in three and a half days."

Patrick's voice went even colder."Your discretion is noted and appreciated, Marshal."

***

"This interview with Takeo Nakamura is part of the investigation in the death of Theodore Simpson Donaldson. Maintain one camera on Engineer Nakamura, one on me and the third on us both." The interview was Claveaud's fifth of the day. He was conducting it in Nakamura's lab/office.

"First question: where were you between 1000 and 1400 two days ago?"

"I was here, studying core sample reports from Shackleton Crater. From 1130 to 1200, I was in the cafeteria having lunch."

"Were your internal cameras or microphones turned on?"

Nakamura shook his head."Cameras no, microphones yes. And before you ask, there was no one in the lab with me at that time. Akane came by around 1030 to ask about a new shaft we may dig out there if we get the chance."

Zach grinned."That's almost as good as a camera. Akane autoposts his entire schedule to the joint website to include every time he walks to a new location, with video."

Takeo nodded in agreement."It's why he's the most popular member of the team back on Earth."

"OK then, next question: did Mr. Donaldson pursue your wife, Bonnie, like he tried with a number of other woman in the Habitat?"

"No. After that public blow-up with Samantha, I carefully explained to Ted that if I even thought he was sniffing after Bonnie, I'd beat him to death and desecrate his corpse so badly that it would be the only thing future generations would remember about him."

"You're sure he believed you?"

"Yes, I explained this to him after he woke up from the chokehold I put him in. I also had a pipe cutter in my hand and his pants were around his ankles."

"That'd do it." Zach nodded in appreciation."You do realize that puts you in the top five suspect list, and I can't use you in the investigation." Takeo was the second of Claveaud's available deputies.

"Of course."

Zachary asked a few more standard questions and then checked Akane Ito's location record (he arrived at 1028). It didn't clear Takeo for the entire time, but it did make him a less likely suspect. Even so, Claveaud used the same sniffer to analyze the air in Takeo's lab/office.

"Thank you, Mr. Nakamura. This terminates the interview." He packed away the camera drone and then turned back to Takeo.

"Anything else you want to ask or say off-record?"

"Bonnie already moved her pot out of our quarters, but you may find traces with that electronic bloodhound of yours."

Claveaud couldn't help but laugh at his so serious friend."Noted. Anything else?"

"Who are my fellow suspects?"

"Mike Eiling and the other husbands except for Frederick York."

"Why does Frack get a pass?"

"He was with Samantha."

"Not much of an alibi."

"It is now. She started keeping digital after what happened with

Ted."

Takeo shuddered."There's not enough bleach on the moon to get that image out of my mind."

"At least you didn't have to actually see it."

Takeo nodded."Why Mike Eiling, though? He was Ted's lapdog."

"Dogs turn on their masters all the time, Takeo." Zachary pointed a finger at the other man."Speaking of turning on people, Mike was bragging about training with you before I tasered him. Since when did you start teaching trade secrets to the stupid?"

Takeo shook his head and smiled ruefully."Mike's idea of training was to learn three katas, four hand strikes, a side kick and then rely on hitting as hard as he could. I was unable to make him understand that force and motion don't always mean speed, which is what he needs to last more than a minute with either of us."

"Try thirty seconds, *mon ami*."

Both men laughed.

***

The next morning, Claveaud checked in with Wetzel after making sure Mike Eiling ate his breakfast.

"Did Geo and Mapping find anything, Frederick?"

"Sorry, Zach. They set up three signal boosters but didn't get anything."

"Are they in trouble for burning air and resources?" Despite it being a criminal investigation, every project still had to answer yes to the question 'Is the end result worth the expenditure of resources?' Only the station commander could authorize excessive use when she thought it necessary.

"Absolutely not! Hiroko determined how to tie your search in with two other projects. Her boss at JAXA may put her up for an award for best use of resources this quarter."

Zach laughed."Glad I could help."

"So what's next?"

"Now I try to find out who had the time and means to dig a really deep hole inside the Habitat and drop a suit down it."

"Are you sure one hasn't already been dug?"

The marshal blinked at Wetzel and then left quickly without

saying anything else.

***

Claveaud confronted Takeo in his lab."Got a minute?"

"Certainly, Zach. I thought the interview yesterday was complete."

"It was, but this is related. Did the advance team or the remote drones find any shafts, vents or cracks that we couldn't use?"

"There were several. That's why tunnel one is asymmetrical to the other three."

"How large are they?"

Takeo turned around, grabbed his pad and called up the habitat diagrams."You do recall it was those remote-controlled mining drones that put us behind schedule before we even landed."

Claveaud nodded."I remember the report. Not enough sensors on the drones or inspections between drilling sessions, right?"

"That and relying too much on explosives. Let's see, I've got four large areas that are too unstable to use. Two of them are barely more than cracks, but they run very deep..."

Zach interrupted."Can you drop a suit down either one of them?"

The mining engineer looked up."So *that's* what this is about." He glanced back at the pad."No, the surface openings are too small. The third area is horizontal, so it doesn't meet your criteria. The fourth is a shaft roughly four to five feet in diameter..." Takeo looked up."...and it's over 120 meters deep."

"That's it! Where can I access it?"

"The hatch is at the end of tunnel one. It's set in the floor, by the right wall."

***

Zachary looked at the vidscreen linked to his drone and shook his head. He stood on a platform about 20 feet below the hatch with a signal booster."Wetzel was right, Gwen. Drop it down a deep enough hole and the signal disappears."

"How are you getting it out?"

"I'll use a mining drone to attach a line to the shoulder hooks and then haul it up with a winch." Claveaud chuckled."This was literally the last place to look."

"To hide the suit that well, it would take someone with extensive knowledge of the remote drilling and other operations before we arrived...or someone with access to the information."

"You sound like you just cracked the case, Gwen. Tell me what you got, oh intrepid girl detective."

"I can determine who was researching this particular area of the base and see if any names match your suspect list."

"I can do that, Gwen."

"Not their personal computers you can't."

The only privacy station personnel had on the moon was their research data and personal computer equipment. Access that was only accomplished by the station commander and that had to be reported to the heads of JAXA and NASA once done.

The space agencies then informed the personnel investigated. They would have the choice of using agency counsel or securing personal representation to determine if the access was valid or not. Depending on the circumstances and the information accessed, a station commander could be removed if the offense was particularly egregious.

"You sure you want to burn that bridge, Gwen?"

"There's been a death on my station, Zach; possibly a murder. I'll do whatever it takes to find out what happened."

"OK, but let me see if I can pull any fingerprints or tissue samples from the suit first. That'll be better than a search history, especially if there's more than one person involved."

"Trying to steal back your thunder, intrepid boy detective?"

"'Boy detective,' *ma chere commandant*? I am a fully trained and vested marshal, so I'll thank you to not interfere in my..." His voice trailed off as he saw something else on the drone's video feed.

"Zach? What is it?"

"A ceramic edged tool with what appears to be a two-inch blade and a guard-less handle. One piece. I guess we've found the murder weapon, Gwen."

"Do you need a witness before you bring it up?"

"That would be good. I've already eliminated Edwin Scott as a suspect."

"Tell Takeo you need one of his drones and I'll send Mr. Scott your way."

***

"Thanks for coming, Edwin."

"I should thank you, Zachary. This is the most exciting thing to happen to me since we landed."

"You get to see a winch pull a suit out of a hole, Edwin. Your definition of exciting is very different from mine."

"Perhaps." Edwin peered at the video feed."There's a claw on this drone, isn't there?"

"Yes, there is. I...so you want to know why we don't just use it to grab the knife while we're waiting for Paul?"

The geologist broadly smiled."If you don't mind of course, Marshal."

"OK then, wise guy, let's see what we get." Zach lowered the drone to an inch above the knife."Claw locked. Let's bring her up."

CRASH! Edwin slammed against Zachary, almost knocking him off his feet and over the edge.

"*Fichu*! Edwin, what happened?"

The older man was desperately trying to cover a large hole in his helmet with one glove while trying to get an emergency patch out of his leg pouch with the other. Adding to the problem was a six-inch bolt lodged in Edwin's helmet that still protruded through the hole.

"Zachary! I have a problem here!"

Claveaud quickly pushed Edwin's hand from the leg pouch and removed the patch. He slammed it against the ground, breaking open the two chemical capsules, and placed it over the damaged helmet. The binary components quickly mixed and congealed into a seal almost as hard as the helmet itself, holding the patch in place.

"Medical emergency!" Comm circuits activated automatically to Sickbay.

"Evans here."

"Doc! I've got Edwin down with a hole in his helmet!"

"Get a patch over it. Where are you?"

"Patch is already on, but he's coughing badly. We're under

Tunnel One and..."

Claveaud noticed that Edwin was bleeding from somewhere on his head.

"There's also a head wound, Doc. I need to get him out of here."

"Can you carry him out?"

"Maybe. Takeo is already on the way with a drone winch if we need it. Just be ready once we're up."

Evans opened a comm link to the chief geologist."Edwin, this is Doctor Evans."

The raspy voice came back almost a whisper."Hello, Doctor."

"Don't speak again until we get you to Sickbay. If you can get to your feet, blink twice at Zachary and let him help you up." Scott did as ordered.

"OK Edwin, you and I, we're gonna take this one step at a time." Claveaud nearly carried him up the steps."That's it. You're almost to the hatch. Grab the lip and pull up. I'll give you a shove if you can't do it yourself."

Claveaud had just cleared the hatch when Takeo arrived. Once Zachary had it secured, Nakamura unsealed the portable airlock around the two men and pulled the front out of the way.

"Get his helmet off, Zach, and we'll carry him to Sickbay."

"No can do. I'm not sure how badly he's bleeding, and that bolt may be lodged in his skull. Let's go." They lifted Edwin up in the astronaut version of a fireman's carry and then leaped him to Sickbay. As they arrived, Paul Nordling came in right behind them with his tool kit. Evans was waiting.

"Put him on the table." The doctor looked down at his patient."Edwin, I'm going to give you three injections. You'll be unconscious before the third one." Once done, he looked up at Claveaud and Nakamura."Paul's going to help get the suit off. You two can't do anything here. If you want to be useful, go find out who did this."

The two men left Sickbay and headed back to the hatch at Tunnel One.

"Zach, Wetzel should already be at the hatch with the winch drone. Before you say it, we'll scan every inch of the hole before trying to lift the suit out."

"Good. I want to find out exactly what it was that nearly killed

Edwin."

***

"What do you mean no DNA, Zach?" Gwen looked ready to pull the top off her desk.

"Whoever wore that suit was prepared. A full skinsuit was worn to prevent leaving any skin cells, sweat or other fluids behind. What smells like peroxide was flushed into the air system. The scrubbers are shot and there's nothing useful anywhere."

"What about what nearly killed Edwin?"

"It's a case-hardened, hollow steel bolt launched out of a tube powered by a CO_2 cartridge." Claveaud waited for that to sink in.

Gwen frowned."That sounds familiar."

"It should. It's one of the tools used to gather samples before we start drilling into new rock. Ted used them extensively to check for radiation."

***

Beep! The ID on the screen display read *Doctor Evans*. Claveaud blinked once at his computer to open the call. It had been a long, sleepless night.

"Yes, Doc. How's Edwin?"

"He's doing fine, Zachary; almost no dust in his lungs, and what turned out to be a deep cut over his left ear. I'll let him out of sickbay tomorrow, but he'll be on light duty for three days."

"Best news all week, Doc; thank you."

"Hold off on the goodwill. I finished my autopsy on Ted, and I can say without a doubt it wasn't murder. He was dead before his suit was compromised."

It took Zachary a moment to process."How do you know that?"

"No damage to his lungs from dust inhalation. Almost no dust in them at all, just like Edwin. Ted had stopped breathing completely before his air supply was contaminated. I should have realized it when we removed his helmet for the autopsy and saw how little dust there was caked around his mouth."

"Are you trying to tell me Ted committed suicide? That's impossible in a suit without setting off an alarm."

"He managed it somehow, Zachary. Paul can probably figure out how he did it."

"Why would he do it, though?"

Evans shrugged."That's more in Dr. Yamamoto's field of expertise. I'll start a forensic check of his medical records in case there's anything I've missed or has been altered. Once that's started, I'll begin a more invasive autopsy."

"Are you certain he died in the suit? He wasn't killed somewhere else and stuffed in?"

The doctor began to look irritated."Yes, cause of death was anoxia and you, I and Paul all know there's no way to shove a body in a spacesuit and make it look natural."

"Thanks, Doc. I'll call Gwen and we can go over Ted's last psych exam together with Kayoko."

***

Nordling called in Zachary the next morning to explain how Ted got around the suit safety precautions. Since Edwin nearly died helping him get the suit back, Claveaud asked him if he wanted to join in after Evans let him out.

"It's so simple, it's elegant. Ted never had oxygen in his airpack to begin with."

"How did he hook it up, then?" Zachary asked.

"He never activated the suit." Paul shook his head."As long as the airpack and suit are not powered, they can be connected without setting off an alarm. I never considered that would be a possible suicide method, since most people would never make it through an airlock cycle before passing out."

The stocky maintenance chief showed them the suit and airpack."I'd say he turned off the suit at the same time someone else turned off the airpack to avoid setting off the emergency beacon. The second person purged it, then reattached it and never turned it back on. It's easy enough after that to damage the coupling and then push the body off a crater edge."

"Why fake an accident?" Edwin asked."Isn't that just as bad?"

Paul shook his head."An accident victim here can be written up as a 'hero' and used in the recruiting drive for future Hab teams. A murder or a suicide sends chills down the backs of both governments."

"Would it be enough to push Habitat Two back far enough to give the Separatist Movement enough time to build support?"

Zachary blew out a breath."Thanks for reminding me of that, Edwin." He shook his head."I should have stayed in New Orleans and worked on the locks."

"Now that I've further ruined your day, Zach, I'll return to my quarters. Doctor Evans put me on light duty for the rest of the week, as you know." The thin geologist departed with a swagger.

"He's going to milk this for all it's worth, isn't he?"

"Wouldn't you, Paul? On the way here, he said that he's going to ask out Hiroko Makiyam at Geography. 'Because after all, Zach, you only live once.'" Both men laughed.

Paul quickly got serious again."He does bring up a good point: how did we get stuck with so many of these 'Moon First' idiots up here in the first place?"

"Politics, pure and simple. Donaldson in particular because his family has a half dozen senators and congressmen in their pocket."

"That's how he got on the Hab team?"

"Not exactly. Ted had the skills necessary as a pilot and a radiation specialist. His politics should have kept him on Earth; same for Bonnie, Mike Eiling and the rest."

"They really can't be serious, Zach."

"I'm sure there are true believers out there. When people like Donaldson are involved, though, follow the money. Somewhere, his family and a handful of others stand to make a ton of money if the moon becomes independent."

***

Gwen looked up from the exam report on her pad."It still doesn't make sense to me, Zach. Dr. Yamamoto says there was no indication that Ted was even mildly depressed, let alone suicidal. Kayoko's the best in her field; she doesn't miss these things. Ted was narcissistic and a pain in the neck, yes, but not depressed."

"Kay actually used the words 'pain in the neck,' Gwen?"

"OK," she sighed,"that's my interpretation."

"Maybe we'll get something from Doc Evans. He's going back over Ted's records again; physicals, blood work-ups, even the xrays of his twisted ankle just before we launched."

"Do you think they've been altered?"

"It's our last possibility for a reason why, Gwen. The doc is running a full forensic check to include getting scans of hard copies. If something's been cooked, he'll find it. How did the personal systems access go?"

"I didn't find anyone researching deep, dark holes in the habitat, if that's what you mean."

Zach looked at her cautiously."From the suddenly happy look on your face, though, I'm guessing you found something just as interesting."

"Sure did; how would you like to know who researched exactly how to make the weapon used on Ted's suit?"

"Why didn't you start with that when I walked into your office?"

"Because it's fun to see you lose that 'laconic Cajun' face of yours." Gwen grinned and motioned all around her."Let's face it, Zachary. It's not like your perpetrator is going anywhere." She began laughing and even slapped the top of her desk while Claveaud sat and stewed.

***

"Thank you for coming in to see me, Bonnie."

"Let's make this quick, Gwen. Oxygen saturation has reached the point that we can expand Greenhouse Two an additional five centimeters this evening."

"Let's hope your team can handle that without you." She leaned her head back slightly."Marshal Claveaud, come on in."

Zachary walked in from the conference room. He and Gwen had decided to do this immediately after she told him Bonnie had researched the weapon and Zach found several ceramic shavings in Greenhouse One that matched it.

"What do you mean 'without me'?"

"Just a moment, Bonnie." He glanced at Gwen."Are you ready, Commander Patrick?"

"Go ahead."

"Doctor Bonnie Essex-Nakamura, you are here to be questioned regarding the suicide of Theodore Simpson Donaldson.

You are now being recorded, and if you wish to engage a legal counsel from Earth, this is the time to ask."

Bonnie shook a bit at Ted's name."No, I've been expecting this since you found the suit. If it means anything, Gwen, I never intended for Edwin to get hurt."

"That booby trap wasn't for show, Bonnie. Who was supposed to get hurt?"

"Oh, who do you think?" She looked over at Zach.

"You shouldn't have hidden it." Claveaud began to explain."If you had just dumped the suit, I wouldn't have had any evidence. I wasn't certain how you got it out there until Kevin told me an hour ago you picked up a pallet of supports and material for the greenhouse expansion right before Paul reported finding Ted. It was easy enough to hide the suit under that and then dump it while everyone is trying to get a look when we brought in Ted's body."

He held up an oxygen mask with an inflatable hood."You used your quarter's emergency mask with your skin suit to keep you breathing and warm long enough to push the suit into the hole, set the booby trap, and get back in time to join the crowd as we brought Ted in."

The botanist just nodded.

"How did Ted convince you to help him cover up his suicide?"

"By asking. Ted was having headaches, so on our last leave before launch, he got a complete work-up from his family physician. The doctor discovered an aneurysm; very tiny but very deep." Bonnie's voice began to rise to a shout."We both believe that any off-world expansion should have the same political autonomy enjoyed by a nation on Earth. By helping him slow the growth of the colony, it would encourage those of us here to become more self-sufficient. The need and desire to become an independent state would have taken a generational leap ahead!"

The chief botanist paused in her rant, but she stood up and moved toward Gwen."That would have been his greatest legacy. I would have been a part of that, and there's nothing Takeo could have done to take it away!"

She was frothing by this point."It was just bad luck that his helmet wasn't damaged as much as it should have been! Even with it, the plan still would have worked if it weren't for this stupid jackbooted pet of yours!"

"Jackboots?" Zach looked at his feet."These are the same station shoes issued to everyone, *chére.*"

"Why didn't you just die in the tunnel collapse like you were supposed to?"

"Obviously he's not as stupid as you thought, Bonnie. He's alive and you got caught." With that, Gwen got up from her chair and waited until the angry scientist took another step forward.

Once she did, the station commander threw a hard left in the other woman's face. The blow broke Bonnie's nose and bounced her off the near wall to fall to the floor, unconscious.

Zachary whistled."Nice punch, Commander Patrick."

She looked up at him and winked."Family tradition."

"After Doc Evans treats her, how long do you want her in the cell?" Zachary walked over to secure the unconscious scientist.

"You said you can automate for three weeks?"

"Yes."

"No need to give her the full treatment. If Evans approves, let her out after 19 days."

Claveaud tried and failed to keep the grin off his face."Your discretion is noted and appreciated, Commander."

***

"So you're now certain it was a suicide that Dr. Essex-Nakamura decided to make look like an accident, Commander Patrick?"

Gwen gave a slight bow to the image on the right side of her conference room flatscreen."That's correct, Prime Minister Oshima. Autopsy and suit examination confirm it."

Several seconds later, the man on the left side of the screen spoke up."But she and her fellow 'Moon First' compatriots deliberately mishandled it to make it appear like someone was covering up a murder?" Despite advances, communication between the moon and Earth still meant response delays.

"I can't prove the others were involved yet, but yes, Mr. President. The idea was to smear the program and hopefully slow us down long enough to let the Separatist movement gain more political clout and momentum before we broke ground on Habitat Two. It also explains why none of them were exactly excited about finding Ted's killer."

"Are you certain Donaldson was part of the planning in this?"

Zachary spoke up."We only have Bonnie's confession to confirm it, President Norris, but I'd say yes. There's nothing in the communications logs, but all planning could have been done on a face-to-face basis. Their clique gets together quite often."

"So what do you have planned for Dr. Essex-Nakamura, Commander Patrick?"

"When she gets out of the jail unit, Prime Minister, Bonnie will spend all non-working hours in an altered single unit that will serve as home confinement. We should see some extensive breakthroughs in botany over the next six months. By that time, she'll be Miss Essex again."

"What if she or someone else in the Separatist contingent complain?" The Prime Minister asked.

"Officially, I'll repost the contract to everyone's duty roster reminding them that this is well within my authority and is not even the maximum punishment I can implement. After all, she admitted to the attempted murder of Edwin Scott."

Gwen drew a deep breath and then blew it out."Unofficially, I'll break her nose again if she so much as sneezes in an insubordinate manner."

Prime Minister Oshima spoke again, this time looking at Zachary."*Māsharu* Claveaud."

"Yes, sir?"

"Will you support us if we decide to call it an accident?"

Zachary scratched his head."I see no reason to hide the suicide, Prime Minister. The very people we want to come here understand the risks, physical and psychological. It won't scare them off."

President Norris replied."We're more worried about support from those people who don't understand the risks. In particular the Earth First idiots who think we have to fix this world before polluting another one."

Claveaud replied to both leaders."Sirs, everyone on the station knows how Ted died and probably half of them know what Bonnie did to interfere with the investigation. Everyone else will know within a day and eventually all of them are going to talk to somebody back on Earth." Zachary hesitated for a moment and then continued."Trying to cover it up will just play into your opposition's game. It might even give them what they wanted in the first place and pull together enough political support to seriously impact when we can get Habitat Two up and running."

Gwen jumped back into the conversation."Gentlemen, I'd like to suggest the following. Go public with the report personally and immediately. Get the jump on your opponents before they have a chance to put together anything other than the half-baked press releases they're probably drafting up right now."

Prime Minister Oshima spoke again."Is it possible that this was a purposeful sacrifice on Donaldson's part?"

Zachary shook his head politely, but couldn't quite keep all of the sarcasm out of his voice."If it had been anyone else here, that might be an option. Not so with Ted. He would have thought himself too important to whatever cause he believed in to sacrifice himself. Dr. Yamamoto believes that Ted either saw or thought he saw an obvious decline in his performance and removed himself before anyone else could and start to pity him. That embarrassment would have been worse to him than actually dying. That it helped a cause he supported was just convenient."

Gwen shot the marshal a look and then responded,"Mr. President, once we're finished here, and with your permission, I'll request Director Austin isolate Ted's medical records at NASA. I'm concerned that if there's someone back at Johnson sympathetic to the Separatists, they might destroy them just to perpetuate the myth of a cover-up."

"Go right ahead, Commander Patrick."

She turned to the Prime Minister's image."With your permission, Prime Minister, I'd like to request that JAXA do the same with any digital and hard copies they may have of Commander Donaldson's medical records."

"I'll handle that request myself, Commander Patrick. Everything will be taken care of before Earth sets in your sky tonight."

"*Arigatogozimasu*. Thank you both."

"If there's nothing else, Commander, I have to get ready for another 'rubber chicken' fundraiser." President Norris looked like he had indigestion already.

"I have a similar commitment as well," replied the Prime Minister.

"Goodnight then, gentlemen," Gwen told them.

"*Bonne nuit, Messieurs.*" Claveaud bowed slightly to Oshima as he spoke.

Once the call was ended, Gwen sat down and looked at Zachary."You're certain it was a good idea to leave out Bonnie's admission of the first attempted murder?"

"Well, it was only mine." He deadpanned as he sat down.

"Do you really think you can hold it over her head until she leaves?" Gwen needed Bonnie to work, but was willing to send her home with the resupply ship due in four months.

"Absolutely!" Zachary responded."With Ted gone and Takeo divorcing her, all Bonnie has left is her work. A second attempted murder charge will get her bounced back to Earth on the next ship, a year ahead of when Habitat One is supposed to be completed. If she wants a legacy now, she'll have to build it all by her lonesome."

He leaned back and continued,"Eventually, Mike and the other Separatists will start to associate with her again and their 'hero' will be our agent."

"Have you figured out how they rigged the Tunnel Three collapse?"

"Not yet, Gwen. There was no trace of explosives, but Edwin and Akane are looking over the material pulled out of the collapse for everything now. If there's anything to find, they'll uncover it."

***

"What do you gentlemen want this evening?" Gwen asked. Wetzel and York were waiting for them outside her office.

York spoke first."We heard you arrested Bonnie in Greenhouse Two and she put up a fight."

"Why is that important?" Zachary asked.

Wetzel jumped in."We just want to make sure she didn't damage any of the hops or ginger plants."

Gwen rolled her eyes in exasperation."It was in my office, not Greenhouse Two. The future of Lunar Gravity Brewing is secure. By this time next year, you should be shipping beer back to Earth at a handsome profit."

The two scientists cheered and leaped at each other to chest bump. Unfortunately, with the lower gravity, they bounced off and slammed each other into the opposite walls.

Gwen looked at Zachary."OK, I get it now. They're Frick and Frack until the day I leave this station."

"Yes ma'am."

THE MUMMIES OF TARA AL BAY

By
Neal Privett

Lieutenant Robert Shayne watched a dust devil whirl about his yard.

The wind appeared out of nowhere and vanished into the great nowhere again with little fanfare. The winds on the moon were soft and pleasant, sometimes barely noticeable, except for the fact that they reminded him of just how lonesome and remote the little town really was.

The winds blew from way out *there*...rolling across untold miles of lunar frontier. Blowing from the far reaches of a star-shadowed desert and the sharp mountain crags that lay like slumbering giants on the horizon. All that territory...most of it unexplored. Beautiful, but ominous, too. Living on the moon was like a waking dream. Things did not seem quite real.

The sand was so silver here. The terrain almost glowed when the distant sun's rays bathed it with light. What a beautiful, but alien, landscape. Shayne's mind was filled with memories of watching the moon from his backyard, a dreamy child in love with space. He had grown up, attended space academy, and became an interstellar soldier, reaching the rank of lieutenant. Then came the news from Washington that there would be a series of moon colonies.

Americans were going to live on the moon. It sounded unbelievable then…as now.

The States in 3001 CE had reached an all-time high in population, so the only logical solution was to look to the stars. Three years later Shayne was part of the military presence in the first moon town: *Tara al Bey*, an ancient name found etched into stone in the far mountains. Though scientists had yet to fully decipher the language of the first moon civilizations, the name had a nice ring to it.

Scientists had invented a machine that altered the moon's gravitational pull, or lack thereof. It sent an invisible field out that mixed with the moon's energies and produced a gravitational field not unlike Earth's. Now colonists could walk on the surface with ease. They could sit on their couches without floating away. They could work outside beneath the stars in their gardens without their tools rising into the air. They could live normal lives.

Scientists had also developed a pill that allowed earthmen to breathe. Somehow science had figured out a way to take the thin atmosphere: its argon-40, helium-4, oxygen, methane, nitrogen, carbon monoxide, carbon dioxide, sodium, and potassium,—and convert it all into some sort of oxygen-based gas for human consumption. At first Shayne was suspicious of this new innovation. It seemed like so much mad science. But soon he came around to it and had been popping a pill every morning like every other inhabitant of the moon.

Science had also created alternate species of plant life that could be grown and harvested in the thin atmosphere and sandy soil, too. Resilient species of potatoes, carrots, beans, wheat and other crops had been successfully grown. They were sprayed twice a day with carbon dioxide-based chemicals that allowed them to breathe and grow to mutated sizes. It was amazing. Enough to feed everyone and even ship some of the abundance back home to help feed the hungry of Earth.

The residue of ancient wine had been discovered in urns at the foot of the mountains and recreated by scientists in the lab. Now the moon colonists drank ancient moon wine with supper and on weekends. There were even a few burgeoning alcoholics. Shayne laughed. Earth had successfully recreated life in its own image.

Tara al Bey sat like a silent stone on the desert of the moon. A moon town with an Earth feel. A couple of hundred miles away, across the mountains, was another Earth town, *New York*. Shayne laughed. Stupid name. A lunar New York City. He had only been there once. They actually had a Times Square. Basically a few blocks lined with some shops and a café. Pretty pathetic if you asked Shayne. A feeble attempt to hold on to Earth culture…Earth ways. When the colonists needed to adjust, to evolve to fit the rugged lifestyle of their new home.

Unlike New York, Tara al Bey was a modern town that looked towards the future…not the past. Its buildings were made of the smooth, soft stone that was being mined from the local mountains. The citizens wore flowing robes, as the moon people once had. Their space suits hung idly in their closets. The townsfolk went about each day with a relaxed attitude. Each day was as fresh as dew and as slow and easy as any desert town on Earth, or off it. The local cuisine was food grown in moon gardens, or fish caught in moon streams. Not the cheap freeze dried stuff brought along in case of emergency.

The "New Yorkers" still lived on freeze dried sirloin. Freeze dried pudding. Freeze dried beans. Shayne and his people ate fresh greens and drank homemade moon wine at night on their porches, as the lush breezes blew into town off the desert.

The colonists of Tara al Bey were more open minded. They had adjusted to moon life. The New Yorkers were still living in the past, still sweltering in the hot exhausts of their rockets. They had not given up their Earth ghosts.

Maybe in time they would learn to.

Lt. Shayne took another sip of his morning coffee. The day was falling gently on the moon. The colonists lived each day beneath a myriad of stars. But somehow, they could tell when morning came, as well as the night's soft arrival.

This was a morning no different from any other. Shayne started his day early, eager to return to his job as second-in-command of the moon's military unit. So far there had been nothing out there to protect the colonies from. The only signs of life were those from ancient times, long dead. A whisper in the wind. A half remembered vision in the distant caves…that could only been seen if you turned your head just right. The ghosts of a people that lived and vanished eons ago…so long ago, in fact, that the very memory of them had almost been lost in the sands of time.

The troops under Shayne's command were basically there to help build and expand the colonies. There was no outward threat to speak of. But humans could not be stranded so far from home, vulnerable and unprotected. So there Shayne remained with his blaster on ready and his men on alert.

The telephone buzzed across the room. Shayne placed his coffee cup on the counter and moved through the living room to the den. The trans-galaxy communication device glowed in the darkness of the early morning room. Shayne snatched it from the receiver just as the ring was fading away. "Yes?"

It was Colonel Jameson. His raspy unwavering military voice boomed from the other end of the phone. "Lt. Shayne? Get down to headquarters immediately. Something has come up. *Pronto.* Understand?"

Shayne sighed. "Yes, sir. Right away, sir."

Shayne hung up the receiver and headed out the door. His boots echoed through the house, the sound bouncing off the carpeted floors and the soft stone walls. The stars almost swirled in the morning breeze as he stepped outside onto the sandy street. His neighbors had not risen yet. The moon was a very agreeable place. None of the Earth hustle and bustle that forced people into early graves. On the moon, people took their time and relaxed more. They worked hard, but everybody knew that there was no place to be fast. So what was the point of rushing?

Shayne made his way down the street, made a left turn on Bradbury Avenue and walked another block, stopping at the front of the office of the Moon Military Unit. He walked up the soft stone steps and into the arched doorway. He moved slowly down the hallway and rapped on the wall outside Colonel Jameson's office. "Come in," a gravelly voice shouted.

Shayne stepped inside the office and saluted his superior.

"Lt. Shayne, an archaeological discovery has been made in the mountains outside of town. You will take three of your best men and act as escort to the expedition as it travels to the site and back."

"A protection assignment?"

"Yes. I don't expect any trouble, but just the same, any contingent traveling so far away from town needs some reassurance. So go home and get your gear together. Report back here at 1100 hours. You will escort a Dr. Carruthers and a Dr. Rodriguez as well as their crew from here to their reported destination in the Rast al Abb Mountains."

"How long will we be gone, sir?"

"At least a week. Maybe longer, according to Dr. Carruthers. If any significant discoveries are made, you could be up there a good solid month."

Shayne sighed. This wasn't exactly what he wanted to hear. But he saluted and walked back home with a few hours to get ready for a possible month away. Luckily he wasn't married. That would be tough.

***

A caravan of jeeps crossed the desert at a swift pace, leaving Tara al Bey far behind. Lt. Shayne placed a man in each jeep with orders to keep watch on the surrounding terrain as they passed through. Shayne rode in the first jeep and leaned back in the seat with his rifle propped against his shoulder. He puffed on a ten dollar cigar; one of the few Earth pleasures he still allowed himself.

The desert was quiet...almost too quiet. Thousands of miles of silver sand rolled in huge bulges all the way to the horizon. Beyond the dark wall was the side of the moon unseen by Earth. They were not going that far, and the knowledge of that fact was a relief to Shayne. He had been to the dark side of the moon, beyond the mountains, back when the first rockets landed. It was too dark there...and too eerie. Shadows became more than shadows and the old memories of the first denizens still haunted that dark region. More so than on this side of the moon. Shayne wanted nothing to do with it. Luckily, the expedition was stopping in the mountains and staying on this side of the range.

They rode for several hours and then the landscape began to rise steadily. The jeeps carried the men and their equipment higher and higher into the craggy mountains. Somewhere up there was a tomb, Carruthers had told Shayne. A long lost, but recently discovered crypt. The final burial place for ancient kings. Somewhere in the dark corners of the tomb was the key to possibly unlocking the mysteries of the original moon people. Archaeologists had been digging here for a long time, and from what they had learned, the moon had once been home to a very intelligent and mystical people. They had invented a form of writing, formed governments, and from what science had discovered, there was plenty of evidence for organized religious practices.

It was all in their written records. Scientists had logged in thousands of hours to crack the strange hieroglyphics on the walls of the ruins and caves that dotted the landscape out here. Ancient lunar races had flourished back when the moon could have possibly been a totally different place. There was plenty of evidence of extinct vegetation and animal life. Some of the fossilized vertebrae, tiny fish-like creatures, had been discovered in the rock of what had once been a sprawling sea. Shayne himself had seen the fossilized feathers from bird creatures that were found by ancient river beds.

The caves and mountains were full of evidence of past civilizations that had had their heyday then vanished into the sands of time. But the answers were still here. Out here in the wastelands of the moon.

And all the expedition had to do was excavate. Long hours of digging and sifting and recording discoveries. The scientists and their crew were doing that, actually. Shayne's only job was to keep watch over them as they worked.

The line of jeeps left the makeshift road and rolled across endless acres of stones and rubble that burst into powder under the weight of the thick tires. The caravan rounded a bend and kept going, straight on beyond sentinel-like boulders that squatted in the sand in groups of three or four.

Below them was the valley. Its immensity was not comprehensible until one reached the top of the mountain and looked down. Shayne smiled to himself. It was incredible up there. He had a view he didn't often get in town. They were almost up there with the stars. He felt as if he could reach out and touch them. The light of the firmament from that vantage point almost seemed warm. The stars swirled and a comet blazed across the sky. And Lt. Shayne knew why he had come to the moon.

The expedition came to a stop a few miles later. The mountain had leveled out. The scientists began to unload their equipment and set up the tents. Shayne and his men helped them, then stepped back and surveyed the area as Carruthers, Rodriguez and the others began the laborious process of unpacking.

The soldiers spread out and covered all the points adjacent to the camp. There was probably nothing to worry about, but then again…

Shayne explored the area, peering behind every boulder…peeking into every nearby crevice. Carruthers stopped what he was doing and called out, "What are you looking for? Little green men?" The other scientists broke out into laughter.

Shayne smiled. "You never can tell, Doc."

Dr. Carruthers gestured at one of the workers and waved another by as they set up the hanging screens to be used for ciphering sifting the veritable tons of sand that would be excavated beginning the next morning. The scientist wiped his hands on his khaki pants and walked over to Shayne. "Would you like to see the tomb?"

Shayne nodded.

"Right this way." Carruthers led him over a rise. Below was a cave. Shane Shayne and Carruthers moved downhill towards the entrance. They stepped out of the weird night and into a lost world.

It was a simple tomb, hewn into the wall of a mountain by ancient hands. The scientist lit a lantern. He gestured for Shayne to wait until the blue flame sprang to life and grew. Then he plunged first into the darkness.

The tomb had been hidden from the eyes of sentient beings for at least three millennia. Maybe more. Shayne's mind pulsated anxiously inside his skull. It was unbelievable, this place. He walked in Dr. Carruthers' footsteps. They were the first expedition of human beings to ever set foot in there. They moved slowly, spellbound, caught up in the silent awe of the ancient tomb.

"We opened the tomb up a scant 24 hours ago. This is the largest tomb ever discovered. The other tombs were very simple…the resting place of commoners. Nothing to them, really. But we feel that this is the burial chamber of a king. We also refer to their kings as *pharaohs* sometimes…has a nice Egyptian ring to it. Actually, there are many similarities between ancient Egypt and this lost race, from what we've learned thus far. No pyramids as of yet, but the moon-kings wielded enormous power, as the kings of ancient Egypt once did back on our planet. They drove chariots, made war, owned slaves that built great structures. Quite an interesting dichotomy parallel."

The scientist talked on. Shayne grinned. He was receiving his own private lecture. "There is much to be gained from this excavation. We notified your superiors immediately and requested your assistance," Carruthers whispered. The solemnity of the crypt caused them to speak softly...possibly out of a sense of deference. Or maybe it was just a wavering uneasiness that seemed to envelop them. The two men moved slowly, walking behind the lantern, which cast a blue glow over all. The light cut a trail for them to follow through the aged darkness.

Carruthers continued to speak softly, almost as if he were afraid of waking the dead. "Of course, it will be some time before we can actually decipher the long dead secrets of this holy place. Who knows what we will learn here?"

"It's amazing," Shayne said.

"Isn't it?"

Shayne glanced around the chamber nervously. His eyes scanned the corners for shadows that moved. His ears strained to hear phantoms that walked or whispered. This was way beyond his realm of experience. "It's just between you and me, sir...but I think this place is beginning to get to me," he laughed."What do you think became of this civilization, though?"

The scientist smiled. "That, Lieutenant, is the million dollar question. We will hopefully have the answer one day soon."

Shayne could feel the sacredness of the pharonic moon-king's final resting place, the undeniable might of the leader who lay interred there. It was in the stale air that hung there in the chamber like a memory. It was in the echoes of silence that almost seemed deafening.

Painted on the walls in simple pictographs were images of the king's former life. Visions of victorious wars, of fishing expeditions in the great moon seas that had dried up eons ago, hunting excursions into the mountains to snag beasts that no longer existed, of birth and death and rebirth. The wall paintings illustrated the king's life: cradle to grave, and then beyond. The last image etched into the stone showed the king's spirit or soul rising from the tomb and into the sky. Above were the sky gods, waiting among the stars to welcome the king's worthy soul into their midst.

"Look at this," Dr. Carruthers said. He gestured at a section of hieroglyphs. There were rows of what appeared to be lizard-like men. Their fanged lips were parted in permanent howls of rage and their clawed hands were raised in defiance and savagery.

"What in the name of..."

Carruthers chuckled. "I couldn't tell you just yet. We've never seen anything like it. Whatever those beasts are...or were...they seem to be attacking some invisible enemy. Perhaps these creatures were servants of the king."

"Why do you say that?"

"Because look at the king sitting in his chariot over there. He's ordering those beasts into battle. They are the king's front line of attack. No doubt about it." Carruthers said as he pointed to a figure carved into the stone that was obviously the king. The regal figure sat in some sort of chariot with a spear raised high as the lizard creatures charged ahead into the fray. The human-like image of the king contrasted greatly with that of his reptilian warriors. Shayne wondered if possibly there had once been a race of reptilian creatures that were eventually enslaved by the anthropomorphic moon people. Or maybe the things fought and served willingly. There was no way to tell yet.

"Horrible looking things," Shayne sneered. "I hope there's not any more of those running around the desert."

"I wouldn't count on it, Lieutenant," Carruthers said. "These hieroglyphs were made over three thousand years ago. Nothing lives that long. Not even on the moon."

Shayne ran his fingers along some deeply etched letters, carved into the stone wall. "What is this?"

"It's some sort of inscription. We haven't cracked it yet. Rodriguez will take a look at it tomorrow. He's an ace with ancient languages."

Shayne held the lantern closer and tried to read the inscription. *"Vraah le Ubtarr va al Bree...Ak al vree al Seek....*It's Greek to me, Doc."

"Not for long," Carruthers smiled.

***

Shayne followed the doctor through the front chamber, past an arched doorway to a back room where the most valuable grave goods were stored; the objects and necessities used by the king in life and likely what the long-dead priests believed their honored leader required for the afterlife and beyond. There was enough dried food for an army. Clothes folded and stored in crates. Statuettes, weapons such as spears and arrows and swords, dice and board games for the king's entertainment, and there in the corner, propped against the wall, were the desiccated mummies of his slaves. They were much taller than an average human. Their dried out corpses were propped against one another, holding each other in place firmly against the walls. Shayne grimaced in disgust. The bodies were likely women, whose sole purpose for existence was for the care and pleasure of their king. The story of their demise was written in their frozen skeletal faces and hollowed stomachs.

Shayne stopped and stared in horror.

"Yes," Dr. Carruthers said solemnly. "They were buried *alive.*"

Slaves who had paid the ultimate price for their loyalty. Next to them were many dozens of mummified soldiers, clad in a strange armor; their spears and shields clutched between shriveled fingers. Helmets that appeared to be constructed of some sort of leather fastened onto a gold-tinged metal donned their skulls. There might have been a hundred of them, lined against the cold wall as if awaiting orders to march. The unusually tall mummies looked down on Shayne through empty eye sockets. It was chilling.

"Come on." Carruthers led the lieutenant farther across the floor of the crypt. He held his lantern high and cast a strange glow on the far side of the tomb where light had not intruded for eons. The lantern gave life to a myriad of shadows that writhed and danced as the two men moved. And there, in the center of the room was the pharaoh's sarcophagus. The sepulcher was honed from the local soft stone, carved by ancient priestly hands into the shape of the king's body. The lantern shining on the king's likeness on the coffin lid made for a weird silhouette against the wall of the cave.

Something about the sight made the blood freeze inside Lt. Shayne's veins.

"Here the old boy is," Carruthers said, his voice shaking. "We plan to open the coffin tomorrow morning, first thing. I doubt that any of us will get any sleep tonight. We are all so excited."

Shayne's insides were quivering. His spine was in deep freeze. His mind was squirming. He spoke before he even thought…and he wondered immediately where the words came from. *"Don't open it."*

Carruthers wheeled around. "What?"

"Don't…open…the coffin. Leave…now."

"Lieutenant…I don't understand…"

Shayne shook his head and tried to clear his vision. "I…something came over me. I don't know what it was. I apologize, Carruthers…."

The scientist was puzzled. "But why don't you want us to open the coffin?"

"Please do…I apologize. I guess it's the musty air in here," Shayne said. He tried to laugh, but he knew that it was a manufactured gesture, easily observable to Carruthers. Looking around, he saw no immediate threat, so he moved towards the entrance of the cave. "I'm going back. See you outside."

"Yes, Lieutenant," Carruthers said as he adjusted his glasses and watched curiously as Shayne left the tomb.

Shayne walked out of the cave and back to camp with his head spinning and his senses reeling. He shook his head and muttered to himself. *"What just happened back there?"*

Before he realized, it was late and time for the wee small hours, bleary-eyed deep space star gazing, two hour naps, and rotating guard duty.

There would be no dawn, for dawn was just an idea lost somewhere in the land of eternal night. Lt. Shayne wouldn't sleep a wink at all anyway. Visions of the tomb haunted him through his watch duty, through his nap breaks, and into the following morning when the others awoke and emerged from their tents, stretching and yawning and fumbling to get their fires going and the coffee started.

***

The other scientist in charge, Rodriguez, gathered some

excavating tools, a lamp, some charcoal, and some thick drawing paper in his leather bag and headed for the tomb. "I am going to get some initial charcoal rubbings of the coffin hieroglyphics before we get started, Dr. Carruthers."

Carruthers nodded and continued with his coffee. Lt. Shayne sat across from Carruthers and watched Rodriguez move towards the cave. He started to rise, but Carruthers stopped him. "Finish your coffee, Lieutenant. Rodriguez will be alright for a few minutes."

Shayne nodded. The strange feeling still resonated in his gut and he found himself debating the opening of the tomb once again. But he remained silent. Perhaps it was some of that old Earth superstition that hung on and clung to his psyche like wet laundry. He couldn't quite put his finger on it, but there was something...*unholy*...about the tomb.

Dr. Rodriguez was a professional archaeologist, a former professor at USC before signing on to be a part of the moon colonization. When he learned that there was ample evidence of ancient cultures that had once thrived on the moon and that archaeologists were needed to study these long dead peoples, he jumped at the chance.

Now he had more work than he could handle. A veritable career that began this very day. One day soon he hoped to help found the first lunar college, where he could continue his teaching, as well as his field studies.

Rodriguez placed his lantern on top of the sepulcher sarcophagus lid and turned the lantern's volume higher until the entire general area was flooded with the soft blue light, which was easy on the eyes, but also very effective. Strange sounds echoed throughout the chamber. Soft fingers of air from outside curled around the sarcophagus and made his hair dance. He glanced back at the opening behind him. This tomb was the eeriest he had ever seen. He had worked in Mayan temples and crypts before. But this place had them beat in the downright scary department. There was something not quite right here. He found it unnerving, but terribly exciting at the same time. Knowing that the military was just outside was a comfort. They could be there in an instant if he called for them. He reached into his pouch and removed a stick of charcoal and unfolded a large piece of paper.

He could not help but brush his hand across the images, carved into the stone so very long ago. The stone was soft and cold and the images spoke to him. Images of the Pharaoh in warfare and posing with his family...his queen and his sons...communing with strange unknown gods. His hand stopped on a word: *Vaal al Vreen*. Rodriguez contemplated the word...no, not a word...a name...the *Pharaoh's* name...

Vaal al Vreen.

Rodriguez saw the name repeated several times on the coffin lid. The name swelled inside his brain and made him dizzy. The words resonated. Echoed. Almost as if something sentient was repeating them over and over in his mind. He glanced around him. The blue light of the lantern was beginning to shimmer. All of a sudden there was a buzzing sound in his ears and he felt faint. The scientist collapsed backwards onto the cold stone floor. Something drew his attention to the pharaoh's sarcophagus. He could not tear his eyes away.

His heart began to beat wildly. The sound resonated painfully like a drum in his ears. What happened next was like a dream. A weird, horrible, inescapable dream.

The coffin lid began to vibrate. Dust fell from the edges, as it moved. Rodriguez lay there, frozen to the spot, trying to decide if this was an illusion or if it was really happening. It was happening. The coffin lid *was* moving.

A grey gray, skeletal hand emerged from within and pushed the lid away. Rodriguez winced as the heavy piece of stone fell to the floor and a deafening crash filled the tomb.

He wanted to scream...to run...but he could not move. Standing erect before him was the pharaoh's living corpse. The thing was at least seven feet tall and it towered over Rodriguez, staring down at him with burning eyes of moon-fire. Its jaws began to creak and move for the first time in ages. Dust fell from its mouth as it tried to speak, but there were no vocal chords to carry its angered voice.

The pharaoh was dressed regally, in flowing robes of faded gold. On its head was a bejeweled and feathered headdress. It reached into its coffin and produced a long sword that still retained a savage gleam after three thousand years. The weapon glowed in the blue light of the lantern as the creature raised it high. It stepped over the side of its coffin and down onto the cold floor, pausing unsteadily for a moment, as if to regain some life back into the muscles that had shriveled and dried out over the many lifetimes spent languishing in the tomb.

Then the thing took three silent steps towards the cowering Rodriguez. It loomed over the interloper and raised its sword defiantly. The Pharaoh would not suffer these defilers of the holy, these fools. Rodriguez could not pull his eyes away from that burning stare. Those horrible eyes. Pits of hate that studied him intently, as if he were an enemy…just before the kill.

The Pharaoh brought the sword down. Rodriguez heard the wind from the sharp blade as it cascaded downwards, towards his waiting throat. For a brief millisecond, he also heard stirrings in the darkness behind the Pharaoh's mummy…the stirrings of a hundred slaves awakening.

Then the darkness came reeling and Rodriguez heard nothing more.

***

Lt. Shayne was standing on a high boulder, looking out across the desert, when the feeling hit him in the gut like a well-placed punch. Something was wrong. He felt it somehow. Something in the tomb was connecting to him. He wheeled around towards the cave and waited anxiously for any sign of trouble. Professor Dr. Carruthers looked up from his coffee and rose slowly. He studied Shayne for a moment, then he picked up a lantern and moved towards the cave. Shayne followed. Both men met in the middle of camp and jogged swiftly to the tomb entrance.

They disappeared inside the darkness.

Carruthers led the way. The men rushed down the first corridor and into the main burial chamber and there they came to an abrupt halt. They hovered there, frozen firmly in their tracks. The gory vision in the blue light of Carruthers' lantern was too much to take. The scientist fell to his knees and vomited violently. Shayne stood there with his hand covering his mouth, moaning and shaking. The sweat appeared from out of nowhere and ran profusely down his face, saturating his uniform. The lieutenant had seen much death, but nothing like this. The scene in the tomb was *savage…twisted.*

Lying there on the stone lid of the king's coffin was the bloody decapitated head of Rodriguez. The eyes stared blankly at a horror they could no longer see, and Shayne wondered what terrible thing the dead man had witnessed just before the end. Rodriguez's headless body lay on its back on the cold stone floor, with both arms outstretched. His tools and lantern lay scattered beside the body.

Lt. Shayne noticed something then. The coffin lid had been *moved*, and subsequently replaced. The dust had been disturbed all around the sepulcher. And there was something else.

Rodriguez had been killed...horribly slaughtered and decapitated by *something*. Yet there was not *a single drop of blood anywhere*...on the coffin...the floor...the body. Wild panic began to seize Shayne, then and he lifted his rifle higher. He began to glance about with a hawk's eye, surveying each dark corner for signs of movement. He reached over and pulled Carruthers close behind him, and the two backed out of the tomb slowly and into the open. Shayne glanced up at the swirling stars above as they ran from the mouth of the cave. For the first time in his life, the stars were not diamond-eyed embers of beauty. The romance and awe he once held for the moon and its firmament was now replaced by a white hot current of fear.

The two men stumbled into camp and collapsed by the nearest campfire. One of the archaeologists helped the men up into sitting positions, then poured two cups of coffee and handed them to Carruthers and Shayne.

Carruthers tried to force a smile. He began to shake uncontrollably. "I...I think we may need something a little stronger than coffee, Ayers."

Ayers sat down beside the older scientist. "What happened in there, Dr. Carruthers?"

Carruthers glanced painfully at Shayne, then back at the others, who had gathered around the fire to listen. "Rodriguez is dead," he said. There was a collective gasp, then a stony silence and a discernible gloom that fell over the camp.

Shayne's men had quietly approached the fire and stood over the archaeologists with their guns raised. The lieutenant took a half-hearted drink of the hot coffee and nodded to them. They moved back to their posts, as silently as they had come. An empty feeling ate away at him and he knew beyond a shadow of a doubt that he should have been in the cave with Rodriguez. If only he had been there to protect him.

Shayne rubbed his eyes. His head throbbed with pain and his stomach burned with nausea. *Damn it.* Why hadn't he gone with Rodriguez? Why did he let him go into the tomb alone? He had failed in his duties. And now a man was dead. There was something pushing him away, some force…something unnatural. The thought of venturing back into the tomb sickened him further. He no longer felt like a soldier. He felt like a superstitious fool.

Ayers studied Carruthers for a long moment and finally found some words lost deep in his fear-dry throat. "What happened?"

Carruthers stared away, deep into the lunar distance, where night never ended. His thoughts were muddled ghosts and every time he believed that he had the anxious nausea quieted deep down in his stomach, it rose once again to strangle him. *"Don't ask me yet."*

Shayne collected himself and placed his cup on the log beside the fire. Never again. No more lost lives. He had to conquer this strange fear that had overtaken him and keep these men safe, at any cost. "Your colleague was killed by an unknown entity. That's all we can say at the moment. And until we know more…that cave is *off limits.*"

Carruthers continued to stare blindly at the stars. But Ayers hopped up in shock and anger. "You can't be serious," he shouted."What about the tomb?"

"The tomb is temporarily closed," Shayne muttered.

Ayers grabbed Carruthers by the arm. "Doctor…please tell the lieutenant that we can't lose even a single day more! This is the find that will literally write the book on lunar pre-history. We can't quit now!"

"I didn't say anything about *quitting,*" Shayne said. "I just said we were going to stay out of the cave until we find whatever killed Rodriguez."

"Why can't we work under guard?"

Shayne rose. "Not until we find out what's in there." Gore soaked visions of Rodriguez oozed across his mind and he clenched his teeth, holding on to his shame as if it might escape. "I should've posted a guard in there with Rodriguez. His death is on me. But we aren't going to have any more. One's enough."

Ayers started to speak, but Shayne raised his hand to silence him. The archaeologist shook his head in disgust and stormed away. The lieutenant sat quietly beside Carruthers. A weird chill enveloped them as they sat together, two men side by side, contemplating the unknown. They watched the fire slowly fade and listened to the beatings of their own phantom hearts.

***

A few hours later, Shayne ordered his men to keep the first watch and collapsed into exhausted slumber for a few hours. He slept restlessly, tossing and turning in his tent as more bloody images of the scientist's mangled corpse returned to haunt his dreams. Then something was in his head, something that caused him to wake violently and bolt upright. He stared blankly ahead into the darkness for a moment while the fog in his brain diminished, then he scrambled through the tent flap. He glanced around quizzically for a few seconds and noticed that his men were doing the same. Something was wrong.

All of a sudden, something moved to his left. Shayne wheeled around to see Carruthers emerge from his tent. The archaeologist's face was mechanical and dream-ridden, as if something was controlling him. He stood in the night air, staring ahead in the direction of the tomb, as if waiting for a command, a beckoning call, from some unknown source.

The lieutenant was about to enquire if everything was alright when Carruthers began moving towards the cave.

"Dr. Carruthers," Shayne shouted."Dr. Carruthers...*wait!*"

Carruthers did not hear. He did not stop. He continued on, drifting silently across the sand like a wayward specter intent on some invisible goal. He was blank and devoid of any cognizance or feeling. It was as if he was walking in his sleep.

Lt. Shayne rushed after him. He motioned for the other soldiers to head the doctor off, but the scientist walked quickly past them and continued over the rise.

"*Carruthers! Stop!*"

Shayne came to a stop on top of the hill and stared in disbelief as Dr. Carruthers walked down the trail and disappeared into the inky darkness of the cave. Shayne's men ran up beside him. "What now, sir?"

Shayne rubbed the disheveled hair on his head and cursed under his breath. "Simms...you and Douglass stay in camp. Carroll...you come with me."

Shayne went back for his rifle and a lantern. Then he led the way into the cave.

The piercing blue glow of the lantern illuminated the first chamber as they rushed inside. Strangely enough, Carruthers had entered the blackness without a light. Shayne held the lantern before him, pushing back the darkness into the far corners. There was no trace of the archaeologist. Shayne's blood temperature dropped several degrees when he considered the fact that Carruthers was somewhere deeper inside the cave..., wandering around in the dark.

The soldiers raced into the king's burial chamber. The air turned even colder suddenly and Shayne handed the lantern to Carroll. Shayne's heartbeat pulsated deep inside his ears and it made him slightly dizzy. But he shook it off. What he couldn't shake off, however, was the haze that came from the other side of the darkness. It made his eyes swim. It made the walls of the cave shimmer.

Carroll felt it, too. "Sir...what's going on?"

Shayne was about to answer, but the words died in his icy throat when he heard the lacerating scrape of the pharaoh's coffin lid as it moved. He jerked his head around so fast that it made his spine pop and creak. The two men stood there, spellbound, as the heavy stone lid fell from the coffin, as if pulled by supernaturally strong and invisible fingers.

There was a scratching sound within the sarcophagus, and then something appeared out of the black...peering over the coffin's edge, trying to force its way into a standing position. Shayne tried to move, tried to raise his rifle, but the muscles in his body were frozen like pipes in a Nebraska winter.

Carroll could not tear his eyes away. Something tall and thin rose from the shadows. It writhed and almost danced in the haunted blue light, reaching into the air in some grim display of rebirth and twisting as if it were a marionette with strings pulled by an unseen master.

The pharaoh, a majestic angel of death, towered before them. Skeletal fingers, longer than an average human's, wrapped around a royal blade that had tasted more blood than Shayne or any of the other moon colonists could hold in their puny mortal bodies.

The great lunar conqueror. The god from distant stars that had died when the moon was but young and a fresh tear in the galaxy's eye. An ancient king returned from the land of the dead, a realm forever unknown to earthlings.

"Lieutenant," Carroll moaned. *"Help me…"*

Before Shayne could move, the pharaoh's mummy vaulted from its stone sarcophagus. The echo of its sandaled feet on the smooth cave floor resonated across the tomb. The thing raised its sword high and the edge of the wicked blade glistened in the lantern glow. There was a lightning flash of movement, and the blade sliced through Carroll's throat like tissue paper. Gouts of deep red blood covered the soldier's face and uniform and his lifeless shell collapsed to the floor.

A flash of adrenaline surged through Shayne's mind as the shock wore off, and he sprang back to life and action. He wheeled around and brought the rifle's muzzle upwards into the face of the living mummy.

But the pharaoh known in life as Vaal al Vreen, was quicker. It caught the muzzle in its clawed hand and jerked the weapon from Shayne's hands. The gun landed beyond the shadows and slid to a halt against the wall. The mummy grabbed Shayne by the throat and lifted him into the air. He was weightless, a mere nothing to this seven foot tall horror from the grave. Every bit of muscle and gristle in the lieutenant's body turned to jelly. Shayne had never felt so helpless before. He was dealing with the supernatural…something beyond Earth earthly understanding, and he was doomed.

The pharaoh brought the bloody end of the sword against Shayne's throat. In another second, the thing would drive the blade home and Shayne would be no more. A thousand memories and images shot through his brain like an out of control celluloid explosion. It dawned on Shayne all of a sudden. It was a pointless death in a place man did not belong.

He gazed deep into the pharaoh's brown, mummified face, that which leered at him from beneath the headdress. The nose was gone. The leathery skin was dried and pulled tight around the high cheekbones. The mouth was a twisted, maniacal smile carved into the skull by the ravages of time. The deserts were dry, and that had helped to preserve the beast for posterity. Its followers probably embalmed it with something, too.

The living dead ruler of an ancient lunar civilization was older than the oldest Egyptian pharaoh back on Earth. It knew things that man could never know or even comprehend. It knew deep time and all the secrets and horrors contained therein. And now it was about to drink Shayne's life essence. Just like it had with Rodriguez.

"Hope you choke on my blood, Your Majesty," Shayne gurgled.

The lieutenant felt the cold edge of the pharaoh's blade slice into him and he winced as the first soft bubbles of blood appeared on his skin. The red began to trickle down his throat. He groaned at the sharp sting.

He stared deeply into black sockets where the king's eyes once were. There was nothing in those empty sockets...just a single spider web. Nothing more. No retinas. No corneas. No pupils. Strangely enough, the creature could still see. The shriveled death's dead head leaned close to Shayne. Their faces were almost touching. The pharaoh studied Shayne. It tilted its head back and forth, right and left, as if it was waiting to see what the helpless earthman would do or say before it plunged the sword deeper into his waiting throat and bathed in his blood.

Shayne did nothing. Maybe that simple fact prolonged his life a few more seconds. Maybe the pharaoh could sense he was a fighting man, too. And if that were the case...then maybe Shayne should go out doing what he did best. Maybe he should give the king what he expected. A fight.

The lieutenant brought his trembling fist up with all the strength and fury he could still muster. His knuckles smashed the dried flesh beneath the mummy's jawbone and he heard it snap. The blow caught the mummy off guard. It dropped Shayne and fell back a couple of steps. It stood there, temporarily dazed, but it did not drop the sword.

Shayne saw the jawbone hanging limply off the side of the pharaoh's face. The mummy was surprised and for a few seconds, it did not know how to react. Shayne doubted it felt any pain, but it damn sure felt shock. And in the next instant, *fury*. The creature lumbered forward, all seven feet of it. A weird howl exploded from its shriveled lips. It raised the mighty sword and took a giant swing at Shayne's head. He ducked and rolled, scrambling after his rifle on the far side of the sepulcher.

Shayne reached the rifle and rolled over, quickly loading a shell into the chamber. He heard the pharaoh's heavy footfalls around the side of the coffin. His fingers slipped once on the rifle, but he shoved another shell in just before the beast reached him. The thing let out another howl, even more hellish than the first.

The blue lamplight reflected once more off the sword blade as the mummy raised it high, over Shayne's skull. It was just about to bring the sword careening down into his head when the lieutenant brought the rifle muzzle up and aimed it directly at the thing's face. There was a loud report, and the ancient moon-king's head separated into a thousand dried out flakes that erupted like a small volcano. Pieces flew off in all directions and the pharaoh fell back. But it didn't go down. It swung blindly with the sword. Shayne crawled backwards in an attempt to escape the headless thing frantically slicing at the air around it.

Shayne rose and cocked the rifle. He aimed and fired again and again. The pharaoh exploded, and after the smoke cleared, there was little more than a pile of golden robes and an empty headdress beneath dust and brittle bones.

The lieutenant fell to his knees. His breaths came in short, panicked gasps of gut-wrenching pain. He sat there on the tomb floor for a moment and tried to cool the fevered flashes of his heart and lungs. "*Sweet God Almighty*," he whispered. His eyes remained on the pile of bones, as if the pharaoh would resuscitate itself at any moment and close in for the kill when the lieutenant least expected it.

But the moon-king remained dead this time. A cool velvet wind blew softly from outside, and Shayne found himself desiring the peace of the stars and a nice cold drink from camp. He rose slowly and limped towards the doorway beyond the front chamber.

Shayne stopped to pick up the overturned lantern on the way out of the burial chamber. And that is when he heard it…the rustling coming from the shadows deeper inside the burial chamber. He turned slowly, his heart a limp; dead thing inside his dried throat. Shayne held the lantern high and peered through the dark, past the pharaoh's bones. He stopped breathing.

In the blue light, shambling like a dozen choice nightmares from a damned soul's psyche, came the pharaoh's mummified servants, shambling forward slowly with their clawed bone-tipped fingers outstretched, raking the air. Terrible moans, never heard by human ears, cut through the stillness of the tomb and white hot shock pilfered filtered through the recesses of Lt. Shayne's mind, followed by a cold wave of fear as it washed over his skin.

Shayne bolted from the cave as fast as his legs would carry him and headed for camp. He stumbled once before he reached the front opening and after that, his memory failed him. The next couple of minutes were lost in a frenzy of animalistic panic until he reached camp and his mental faculties returned to him slowly.

Shayne called out, but no one answered.

The lieutenant moved closer, with his rifle raised and ready to fire. He moved over the rise and stopped just before the archaeologist's tent. "Ayers…Ayers…are you there?"

No answer.

Shayne moved towards the center of camp and called out to his men. "Sims! Douglass! Respond on the double!"

There was only the sound of the wind brushing against rocks more ancient than time itself. Shayne started to feel the panic welling up from deep inside his gut again. Something was wrong. He called out again.

Nothing.

He moved cautiously through the camp and stopped when he saw the boot behind the soldiers' tent. He rushed around behind it and placed the lantern on a rock. It was Simms. He was white as moon sand, and at first Shayne thought that he was grinning from ear to ear. The shadows were thick and he couldn't tell for sure. But when he held the lantern closer, he realized that there was a savage gash in his throat. Shayne stood over his fallen comrade, trying to make sense of things.

Then it hit him. There was no blood. No blood around the wound…on the body anywhere. None on the sand beneath Simms.

Shayne glanced behind him and saw the archaeologist, Ayers, lying on his stomach. He move closer and examined the corpse. Something had torn the eyes from Ayer's head. Ripped his tongue from his mouth. Slashed his throat.

But there was no blood.

He glanced around frantically. There was no sign of Douglass or the other workers. He turned to look at Simms again. He studied the ground around his body. There had been no sign of a struggle. Something had appeared out of nowhere and killed Simms instantly. And sucked every drop of blood from his body.

Shayne shuddered when he saw the dead glare in Simms' eyes. There was a tinge of faint surprise around the pupils. Maybe he had seen someone he recognized. He scratched his chin and wracked his thoughts. Then a possibility crossed his mind, and he didn't like what he was thinking.

"Not a pretty sight, is it, Lieutenant?"

The sudden sound of the voice from the darkness made Shayne jump. He wheeled around and aimed his rifle at the shadows. Then a face appeared in the blue light of the lantern. A face that was instantly familiar.

"Carruthers! Where have you been?"

Carruthers moved into the light. Shayne noticed the blood-caked wound on his forehead right away. "Do not be afraid, Lieutenant," the scientist said. His voice was slow and almost monotone. He walked as if there was no feeling in his legs. He stared straight ahead as he spoke, as if he could not see.

Shayne held his rifle close. "Carruthers…there is something evil in that tomb. Carroll is dead. It almost got me, too. We have to leave…"

"We should never have come here in the first place," Carruthers said with a strange smile. "We are not wanted here."

Shayne stared at the scientist in disbelief. "Carruthers…your eyes…"

Carruthers' eyes were demonic. They were glazed over and milky. There were no pupils. It was as if he were blind. "I understand now, Shayne. I didn't at first…but now I do."

"Understand what?"

"The hieroglyphs we found that day…the ones that translated as, *Beware interlopers…the king is as timeless as the desert and as formless as the heavens. He shall not stop in his vengeance. He shall escape the dust of his bones and find a willing host…then he shall drink of the blood of the living until the last trespasser is gone…*"

"The Pharaoh's mummy is *dead*...I killed it!"

"Vaal al Vreen cannot die," Carruthers laughed. "You destroyed his body but not his spirit. The Pharaoh now resides in me...and I will do his bidding..."

"...*until the last trespasser is gone*. Eh, Carruthers?"

"Exactly," the scientist said. "Now don't fight it, Lieutenant...this won't hurt..."

Shayne shoved the barrel of his rifle into Carruthers' ribs and pulled the trigger. The archaeologist's torso spread apart like a fevered dream in slow motion. When Shayne stepped back, there was a gaping hole in the center of him. Carruthers lumbered toward Shayne with a single intestine dragging the ground. The scientist was possessed with the life essence, the soul, of the pharaoh, and he began to speak in the old tongue as he lunged at the lieutenant. "*Vaal al Vreen al shay. Vrook ja hem shay...*"

The scientist grabbed at Shayne with both arms outstretched, but the lieutenant ducked and brought the butt of his rifle up against his skull, shattering the bone into splinters that rose beneath the skin. But Carruthers kept coming. His eyes had taken on an otherworldly glow and his voice had become a low scratchy dirge straight from the tombs.

Shayne hit Carruthers with the butt of his rifle again. He tried to move backwards, but the scientist was stronger and faster with the blood of his comrades inside him...just as the hieroglyphs had promised. Before Shayne could react, the thing grappled him with both arms and lifted him up into the air. His grip was deadly. His arms were like two steel bands. There was nothing Shayne could do but try to keep the breath flowing in and out of his lungs.

The creature that had once been Dr.Carruthers, eminent archaeologist, was now a raving, undead beast with a sacred blood mission to quell the infidel flames that had been kindled the moment Vaal al Vreen's tomb had been desecrated. Shayne gasped and struggled against the supernatural death machine to little avail as it tightened its grip on his torso and squeezed until Shayne could taste the blood rising into his mouth.

Shayne kicked back and threw forward his head with all the might he could muster and drove Carruthers' nose deep into his possessed brain. The pharaoh's host took a few steps back. A long, dark stream of blood ran from the collapsed nostrils, but Carruthers did not let Shayne free. However, the thing's grip loosened just enough to allow Shayne another direct hit to its face, causing the thing to release him.

Lt. Shayne hit the ground, rolled over and quickly grabbed the rifle. He shoved another cartridge in and aimed for the beast's eyes. The campsite was rocked by the deafening report and Carruthers' head disconnected from his shoulders. The thing took a few more steps forward, reaching for Shayne blindly, before collapsing to the ground in a bloody heap.

The moon returned to silence then, and Shayne fell to his knees. He sat there reveling in that silence for a long time. He gazed upwards into the infinite stars and thanked every single one personally for his life.

The air took on a clammy chill as he paused to look down at the cave entrance. He could still hear the slow rustlings of walking corpses roaming the dark corners of the tomb. The entrance had to be closed, he knew, blasted into rubble so nothing could ever emerge from the tombs again. Shayne took the case of explosives from under the seat of the jeep and placed the rifle in the backseat. He took a roll of wire and the case and raced down the hill to the cave. After he tightened the clamps down around the wire ends, he set the timer for ninety seconds and sprinted back to the jeep. There was a great explosion that rocked the camp and the mountain collapsed, covering the tomb entrance once again.

Shayne blew a sigh of relief. He watched the dust settle below, then turned back to the jeep. He found the keys waiting in the ignition.

***

The lunar-outfitted vehicle sprang to life with a turn of the key, and Shayne rolled down the rocky slope to the sprawling valley below. He kept the twin killers of panic and horror suppressed way down in his gullet and he drove as fast as the jeep would take him. The winds were gentle and cool, and Shayne knew that night had descended on the moon. At least in terms of time. The sun never rose or set here, but he could feel when evening rolled in.

There was a flash in the sky. Shayne looked up to see a comet soar over the landscape, then vanish. For a moment, he found himself wanting to drop out of the army and build a tiny house way out in the desert, escape the moon colonies for good. Live out the remainder of his life out of uniform and totally alone. He had left something back there in the rubble of the tomb. What, he couldn't quite put a finger on. But what he did know now was that it was wrong. All of it. He shouldn't be here. They would have to understand. All of them. The people of Tara al Bey *and* New York. The people coming on other rockets. They would all have to return to Earth. The moon was no place to colonize.

There was an evil here older than man. And it would never allow them to live in peace now. This was not their land. Earthlings did not belong on the moon.

The mountains were not so far behind when something odd happened. There was an explosion of sand far off to the right. Shayne glanced out into the starlit expanse, but everything was still. He thought for a second that he had imagined it, but another blast of sand rose in the desert, then quickly disappeared.

Shayne stiffened and grasped the wheel tighter. He touched the rifle in the seat beside him, just for reassurance. He pressed his boot harder on the gas pedal. The jeep sailed off across the sand.

Another explosion of sand. Shayne shot a second glance out at the desert. Something was wrong. Another explosion, this one closer to the vehicle. Shayne grabbed the rifle and held it in the crook of his arm. He had the accelerator pushed flat on the floor. Wind tore through the open cab of the jeep and dropped tiny sand particles that stung Shayne's face and neck. The jeep was going as fast as it possibly could, but it wasn't fast enough.

There was another surge of sand out in the desert, and another. Shayne gritted his teeth and drove like a madman. All of a sudden something was there with him. A dark, hulking shadow ran alongside the jeep. Before Shayne could react, something hit the jeep hard, and the vehicle skidded off to the right. Shayne tried to keep the jeep from flipping. He turned the wheel to the left gradually and tried to keep control. Great sheets of sand flew up and hit him in the eyes, blinding him.

An inhuman roar emerged from somewhere amidst the chaos, and a chorus of beastly howls joined in. The desert was filled with the awful sound. Shayne screamed and jerked the wheel and the jeep was back on the road again. The fear was crippling, but the lieutenant kept driving.

Shayne could hear the sound of great footfalls…something huge running up behind him. He braced himself, with both hands on the wheel. There was a second's pause, as if a storm was about to hit, then a fantastic impact that rocked Shayne and nearly forced him out of the seat. He lost control of the jeep again and swerved off the road, narrowly missing a boulder.

Back on the road again, Shayne peered nervously through the rear view mirror…and what he saw chilled his soul. A huge *reptile* pounced upon the boulder he had just avoided and launched itself skyward with its two muscled, coil-like, legs. Shayne was helpless. All he could do was watch in stark horror as the beast sailed through the air, closer and closer…a terrible lizard silhouetted against a starry sky.

The thing landed on the back of the jeep. There was a terrific groan and apocalyptic grind of breaking glass and twisting metal. Shayne ceased to be a man at that moment and had no more control over himself and his destiny than a bug in a tornado. He flew through the air and landed in the sand several yards away. The lieutenant lay there, with the world a blur and every fiber of his being an aching mass of muscle and tissue that would not respond to his reeling brain's hopeless commands.

He struggled to keep his fluttering eyelids open. To pass out now meant his death. Slowly he raised his throbbing head. His mind was a muddled fogbank. There were several of the things and they moved towards him cautiously, studying him. Shayne figured there was a good solid dozen. They were lizards, but humanoid. Their scaly bodies were thick and muscular. A dark silver, maybe with a hint of gold…the color of the moon. Their faces were full of fangs dripping saliva and their snouts lay flat on their faces. They looked *human*, almost, and they stared without as much as a drop of mercy in their glimmering yellow eyes at Shayne, lying vulnerable and broken on the roadway.

Shayne knew beyond the shadow of a doubt that he was a dead man.

Then it hit him. Shayne remembered the crude drawings on the cave wall. These were the unholy servants of the pharaoh. The subjugated race of creatures enslaved by the moon-king and his legions. These were the workers and the last line of defense for the old kingdom. Interlopers would not leave here alive. The king made sure of that.

Shayne closed his eyes and lay his head down in the sand. *"I give up,"* he muttered, his voice a hoarse whisper. No one would miss him anyway. His file would be stamped MIA and that would be that.

He could feel the ground vibrating with every forward step those creatures took. He raised his head again and groaned. There would be search parties. Other soldiers would venture up there, to the tomb, looking for Shayne and the others. And they would *die*. He couldn't let that happen. He pushed himself up with his arms. The pain was unbearable, but he had to get out of there, warn the others.

He was on his knees. The beasts…those *moon-demons*…stood there patiently, waiting for him to make it to his feet. Their claws were unusually long.…Too long for their bodies. Those dagger-like fingers could rip open a metal door. Shayne knew they could make short work of him. They grinned, and the saliva pooled around their razor sharp teeth, dripping onto the sand. They were *enjoying* this. They hoped he would run, so they could have the sport of chasing him down.

Lt. Shayne was on his feet now. He took a step forward, and when he did, those things followed his lead. The pain in his back and legs was terrible, but he took another step and tried to put the gnawing ache out of his mind. He glanced around for his gun, but it was nowhere to be seen. Not that it would do any good anyway against twelve or more of these things. But it would have been nice to have had it in his hands. A soldier feels all alone without his rifle.

Shayne took another step and another and broke out into a slow, torturous jog. He moaned in pain as he moved, but he continued on down the road to Tara al Bey. The demons might get him, but they would have to catch him first.

Shayne laughed. *And they damn well would.*

The monsters followed behind him, taking their time. They were going to let him *think* he was escaping. Let him toil and struggle for a few more minutes, then they would pounce on him and that would be that.

The cruel bastards.

Their bloodlust was so strong that Shayne could feel it.

Shayne hobbled down the road. When he got some feeling back in his legs, he picked up the pace, and when he did, those things did, too. They began to howl and jeer. Shayne shuddered and tried to block the awful noise out of his ears. He knew what hell sounded like now. In just a moment, he would know what it *felt* like, too…

Something appeared suddenly on the horizon. It emerged out of the low-lying, star-laden sky and headed towards them. Headlights.

Then Shayne remembered. It was one of the late night trucks that carried goods and supplies from Earth town to Earth town. Tara al Bey to New York. Sometimes, when there was a rocket, the trucks moved supplies, often taking all night long. The driver was on his night route.

Shayne glanced over his shoulder and wondered if the beasts had noticed the approaching truck yet. He seemed to be the sole focus of their attention. He wracked his brain, trying to decide what his next move would be. This was his only chance of making it, but those things would never allow him to climb into the truck and escape.

The truck was closer now. The headlights were like two cat eyes appearing out of the darkness. The lizard creatures saw it. Shayne could feel their hot breath. Their bloodcurdling howls split his ears apart and he cupped his hands over his head, trying to shut the horrible sound out.

The driver leaned on the horn and began to slow down. He was going to be in for the shock of his life. Lt. Shayne waved his arms, and in one last-ditch effort of survival, he mustered every ounce of strength he could and sprinted for the truck with the beasts hot on his heels. The truck rolled forward and Shayne leaped for the side step. The driver leaned over and opened the door. Shayne grabbed the handrail and pulled himself up into the seat, just as one of those things raked his leg with its enormous claws. The driver didn't wait for orders. He threw the truck into gear and took off.

Searing pain shot through Shayne's leg and he screamed. Another demon leaped up on the step after him and Shayne punched it in the teeth. It fell and landed on its back in the sand. Two more of them pounced onto the truck. One of them shoved its arm through the open passenger window and grabbed Shayne by the shirt. All of a sudden there was the loud report of a gun and Shayne glanced over to see the driver aiming a smoking pistol at the thing's face. The beast clutched at its eyes and plummeted from off the moving truck. It slammed onto the road and rolled a few times in a cloud of dust behind them.

Another one tried to get at the driver, but the man shoved the pistol in its mouth and pulled the trigger. The beast's face exploded and it fell away from the cab, but it ripped the door from the hinges on its way out. Shayne heard the impact of the metal door on the road behind them.

The moon demons were fast…like lightning fired from a cannon. The others raced alongside the truck and took turns slamming into the cab and the trailer. With every running lunge, the entire truck shook violently. The driver was doing all he could do to hold on to the wheel and stay on the road.

The driver looked at Shayne. "What are these things, Lieutenant?"

"Would you believe the guardians of an ancient moon-king?"

The driver ran his fingers through his tussled hair. "*What*?"

One of them leaped through the air and landed on the hood. It drew its massive arm back and smashed the windshield with all it had. A slender fissure formed in the center of the glass and traveled vertically up the windshield before it stopped. The beast was about to strike the glass again when the driver swerved sharply and threw the beast from the front of the truck.

"Get on your radio," Shayne said. "Alert the troops in town. They need to be ready with some massive firepower when we get there."

The driver grabbed the transmitter from the dash and made the call in to Tara al Bey. The truck screamed into the town with a throng of wailing demons in tow. They were met with a line of armed troops and a steady barrage of bullets that pushed them back into the desert.

The things rushed the soldiers that blocked the main street and prevented the creatures from making their way into the populated areas. The driver peered from behind the cracked windshield and gasped as one of the things seized a soldier and lifted him into the air. The reptilian horror sank its fangs into the helpless soldier's chest and drank deep from the man's blood before a shell exploded at its feet and knocked it flat. The others did not get that close. The soldiers formed a tight line and pummeled the monsters until they were either gory piles of flesh or they retreated into the desert.

Lt. Shayne hopped from the truck and limped into headquarters, right into the colonel's office. The men watched in awe as he passed them. A trail of blood followed Shayne down the marble floored hall. His leg wound needed stitches. He would have to visit the infirmary after reporting in.

He knew exactly what his report was going to be.

His superior commander stood before the window with his back to Shayne, watching the aftermath of the fight outside. "Welcome home, soldier."

"Thank you, sir," Shayne said as he halfheartedly saluted. "Colonel...with your permission..."

"By all means."

"Colonel...I am the only survivor from the expedition into the mountains. We don't belong here. *Earth* doesn't belong here. We found something up there that we can't explain. Things beyond the pale of our imaginations." Shayne leaned on the desk in front of him. He felt his head begin to swim. He was about to pass out. His heart began to beat faster and the blood in his veins began to surge like ice in a frozen river. "We don't belong here, sir. The moon is *death...*"

The colonel turned from the window to face Shayne. His skin was an ashen grey, and his eyes were clouded, glowing beacons from a lost world. A sardonic smile ripped across the colonel's face, and his raspy voice resonated like shovelfuls of sand heaped upon an open grave. "*Vraah le Ubtarr va al Bree...Ak al vree al Seek...,*" he said as he reached into the desk drawer and produced a pistol, aiming it calmly at Shayne's face. "*I agree, completely, Lieutenant...*"

MISSING

By
John Holmes

Colonel Robert Moore walked to a table where a coffee pot was filling the room with its rich aroma and gurgled, trying to suck in the last of the water. The white tablecloth under it was spotted with coffee stains and spilled sugar. Moore grabbed two mugs. He pulled out the glass pot and filled the mugs.

"What would I ever do without you," he murmured as he breathed the thick coffee smell.

He put the pot back on the warmer, picked up the two nearly full mugs and walked over to his second in command, Captain Ji Sun.

"Here," he offered, holding out one of the mugs to Sun.

"Thank you, sir," she said.

She took the mug with both hands. Sun took a timid sip of the mug's hot contents. She hovered over the mug, stray strands of raven black hair framing her delicate face.

"Think nothing of it," Moore replied, running a hand through his hair, hair that was now more silver than blond, though the sharp military haircut helped hide the fact.

Moore sat in the leather chair across from Sun, sipping his coffee. As he drank the bitter brew, he saw the tremor in her hands and the dark circles under her bloodshot eyes.

"Captain, when was the last time you slept?" he said.

She sat there for a few second longer before answering."My apologies, sir. I've been without sleep for a while and I must have checked out. What was your question?" she asked.

Shaking his head, he sipped some more coffee."Okay, what do you have for me?"

Sun put the half empty mug on the table and picked up her computer pad. She tapped on it and the screen lit up, showing a field of wildflowers gently blowing in the breeze. Up on the right corner was a circle asking for security clearance. Sun typed in her ID code then placed her index finger in the circle. A picture of a woman appeared. Sun tapped it again and looked up.

"I sent a copy to you, sir," she said and started her report.

"At 2309, homes security gets a call from Mr. Brian Jones for a missing person. Investigator Miller and Johnson of SIS (Security Investigator Section) were dispatched. At 2340, homes investigators arrived at the residence and interviewed the husband. Mrs. Betty Jones, married, no kids, twenty-eight, brown hair, brown eyes, no marks or scars. Mrs. Jones reported to Kennedy Hospital at 0600 hours where she is employed as a RN. At 1130 hours, she had lunch with friends. 1400 hours, she left for home. Mr. Brian Jones got home at 1836 hours. Mrs. Jones was not home. At 2115 hours, he still had not heard from her, so he called her cell phone. It goes to voicemail. At 2121 hours, He called the hospital. She wasn't there. At 2139 hours, he tries her cell phone again and it goes to voice mail. At 2145 hours, he call friends, but they have not seen her. He went out at 2154 hours to look for her and doesn't find her. At 2236 hours, he phoned again, but this time the phone is disconnected. At 2309 hours, we get a call from a scared husband."

Sun looked up at Moore."I personally checked all airlocks, all security cameras, computers, and all of the spacesuits are accounted for. Same as before, we have nothing! I still have people out looking for her, but it has turned up nothing."

Moore leaned back in his chair, rubbing his eyes with a forefinger and thumb."Those who have worked over twenty hours are to go home for a ten-hour rest, and that goes for you, too, captain."

Sun opened her mouth but Moore slashed a hand in front of himself, cutting off her protest, arguments Captain."As you head back to your quarters, send Lieutenant Evans over to the computer lab. I want to know if the security cameras have been hacked or tampered with, and to ask if they can beef up the security locks in the building. Any questions?"

Sun shook her head."No, sir."

"Dismissed, Captain."

She picked up her pad and left.

Moore drank the last of his coffee and sat the empty mug on the table beside him. In his lap, his computer pad chirped for an incoming call. He picked up his pad to see Linda Hardcastle, the base general manager, on the screen. She works for the home office in England, and handles the moon base and Mars colonies. She, along with Moore, arrived on base Armstrong when construction was underway, and they worked well together. He touched answer and her face filled the screen. Her red hair was twisted into a bun, held in place by two chopsticks. Moore smiled at the face.

"You're up early. What can I do for you, Linda?"

"Good morning to you, too, Robert," Linda answered."I couldn't sleep after your first report, so here I am."

Moore's fingers flew over his pad's keyboard."I'm sending you everything I have now, Linda."

He watched Linda for a few minutes as she read the report. Moore set his computer pad down on the table and stood up with his hands above his head, stretching to his right and left. He picked up his pad and mug, and walked over to the coffee table. After filling his mug with fresh coffee, Moore went to his desk; he pulled out a black chair and sat down. Moore glanced at the screen and saw Linda was still reading. He turned to his right and brought the keyboard to him. He entered his code and Linda appeared on screen. Moore picked up his mug and sat back in his chair, looking to Linda as she rubbed her temples. She looked up.

"This is not good, Robert. He's gotten more violent with the last three people he's taken."

Moore put his mug down."Linda, this goes no further, but we think that there are two different people and assailants, not just one."

Linda's face paled as she put a trembling hand to her mouth."Do you know for sure, Robert? Please, tell me, not two of them."

"I'm afraid so; the investigators working on this case are two of the best and they have evidence to prove it. The one who took the first three left us nothing, no security scans, no fingerprints, nothing. But, the second one did leave us a lot: blood, some clothing, and a victim's bag with one shoe. Hell, we even have some blood and hair from him. He's not in the system. The detectives are certain they do not know each other and we still don't know how they're transporting them. So when I find out more, you will be the first to know."

Linda shook her head and reached down to her right. Moore heard a drawer open and Linda brought out a bottle that she opened. Taking out two capsules, she dropped the bottle back and popped the capsules in her mouth, washing it down with what was left in her cup. Putting her cup down, she looked up at Moore.

"Bloody hell, this just gets better and better. Robert, you know all the construction is completed for the cities from levels two to nine. Next month the families will be arriving here to start their new lives. I don't want to think what might happen."

Moore could hear the fear in her voice and see it on her face and in her eyes. Keeping his voice even with confidence, he said,"We will get them Linda, before the families get here."

"I know you will, but I'm catching a lot of flak from the home office in England about this and they want answers, Robert. I hate to say this to you, but you have a leak and you need to find it fast, or we will not have jobs much longer. I will back you up all I can, but I can only do it for so long. Sorry."

Moore's face turned red."Damn. When I find whoever is doing this, they'll be brought up on charges! I will not have a traitor in my command, and that I guarantee. Thank you for telling me this. I appreciate it."

"You're quite welcome and I will see you at 0900 for the security briefing." Before Moore could answer, Linda's computer started beeping for an incoming call."Damn, I have to answer this. It's the home office. Call you back."

Moore sat there for a few minutes, rubbing his face."That conversation will not be good."

Moore was about to get up when Mary Ann Lincoln came storming into his office. He saw right off she was not happy. Her eyebrows were pushed together, eyes darkened with anger, and lips in a thin line. He cursed under his breath."Well hell, now what?"

Mary Ann stopped at his desk and held up a slip of paper."I found this on my desk when I came in," she said, sending the paper onto his desk."And I found this computer chip on top." She put the chip down on the paper.

Moore looked down at the paper and chip, then back at her."Well, good morning to you, Mary Ann. Kind of early."

Mary Ann pointed a finger at him and said,"Don't you good morning me. You have been here since 0300 hours." She pointed at the paper and chip."That was not on my desk when I left last night."

He looked back at the paper and chip."This is not the way to start a morning. You looked at all security feeds and checked all computer locks."

"Yes, sir. Nothing. And you were in your office all by yourself. I bet you didn't even know what was going on in my office. Colonel, instead of leaving that note and chip, they could as easily had you."

Moore's face turned pale and an icy cold shiver ran down his back. He mumbled,"Damn, that's not a pleasant thought."

"No, not a pleasant thought indeed. They can come and go without leaving any trace. I checked the front desk. Everybody was where they were supposed to be." She folded her arms and said in a concerned voice."Colonel, if it leaks out that somebody got access to this building and to your office, that's not good, especially with the six missing people. Sir, you could lose your command over this."

"I'm aware of this, but you're not going to like what I have to share." He told her about the leak."Linda is doing all she can. We have to get this problem solved fast."

"Well hell, this just gets better by the minute. Robert, you might want to look at the note," she said, tapping her finger on the note.

He looked at her for a few seconds."Ah hell, Mary Ann," and picked up the paper. As he read it, his eyes started getting bigger. He stopped."This is not real."

"Oh, it's real all right." Mary Ann said. shaking her head.

Not believing it, Moore read it aloud."Colonel Moore, the

computer chip has the information that you will need to find the men who are kidnapping those poor people. The two males are dead. The female will not survive much longer, so please hurry. Signed, a friend."

Moore put the paper down and rubbed his face."I don't believe this. I take it you checked this out?" he said, holding up the computer chip.

"Hell, no. It could have a virus and could crash our whole system."

Moore spread his hand in front of him."Okay, okay. Do we have anybody who can?"

"No, sir. The people we have are good, but not for this," she answered.

Moore rubbed his eyes."All right, we need to keep this in house. I don't want to get the computer lab involved if I don't have to, and it will take too long to have somebody brought up from Earth. Tell me you know somebody, Mary Ann, please."

She smiled and said,"I might know somebody. Well, I mean, Lieutenant Evans told me about her when I was trying to get my personal laptop fixed. She's quite good."

Moore Leaned over and pressed the call button."Call Lieutenant Evans." It rang twice and then he answered.

"Lieutenant Evans here. Good morning, Colonel, what can I do for you, sir?"

"Morning, Lieutenant. Have you started for the computer lab?"

"No, sir. I called and nobody will be there till 0800 hours. Only the night shift is there and the supervisor said we have to make an appointment. Sorry, sir."

"No problem, the sergeant major said that you know somebody who's very good with computers. So, lieutenant, just how good is she?" said Moore.

"She's very good, sir. I met her in Japan when I was on special assignment a few years ago. Her name is Hitoml Ayano; she was top of her class with several degrees in computer science and engineering and has four patents. There was a scandal at college, but she proved her innocence. Unfortunately for her, they were members of very powerful families, so they made sure she was blackballed. When the jobs on the moon opened up, she put in her application, but nobody would even talk to her. Some friends from the United States told her about the waste plant here and they could get her on as a computer tech. She said yes and here she is on the moon. Talk about a waste of talent. Would you like me to get her, Colonel?" said Evans.

Moore looked up at Mary Ann, who shrugged her shoulders."Yes, lieutenant, I do. I don't care what her night supervisor says, or even her boss. I want her here now and I need her full name again for a security check."

"It's Hitoml Ayano, but she likes Jessie. Will there be anything else, Colonel?"

"No, lieutenant," Moore said, ending the call.

Mary Ann headed for the door."l will run a security check and let you know what I find."

Holding up the computer chip, Moore studied it, and then the note. Shaking his head, he looked up when his computer beeped twice and Linda's image popped up and said,"Answer."

Linda's face appeared and she was not happy. Moore could see a slightly red face and a thin mouth. *Damn, this is not good*, he thought.

"How bad is it, Linda?" Moore said.

"Do we have a secure line?" asked Linda.

Moore was surprised by the question."Yes. What's going on?"

"David Blackman called me from the Home Office in England. His boss sent him a report. Robert, it's similar to the one you sent me just a half hour ago."

"Damn, I just got that report twenty minutes before you called and I don't think Sun had time to put it in the system yet. Let me check." His fingers flew over the keyboard and the case file came up. He studied it and said in a grave tone."Yes, I was right. Sun didn't put this report in yet, so this means our system is corrupt along with our computer. Linda, it didn't mention the two different kidnappers?" Ask Moore.

"No, it does not."

Moore setback relieved."Well, at least we have some luck. They only got what was in the system, so much for having a secure system, dammit."

Linda leaned back in her chair and crossed her arms."Sorry about the bad news, Robert."

"I will deal with it, so don't worry, but I have some good news.

I think we have a lead." Moore told Linda about the computer chip and the note. Linda's mouth dropped open in stunned silence.

Then she started laughing."Sorry but that sounds like a bloody cheap mystery novel. I'm sorry, Robert."

"I know. I thought the same thing, but it's a lead and it's the only one we have."

"Do you think it's any good, Robert?"

"I don't know, I should know by tonight."

"I hope so. We need some luck to go our way. Call me when you know anything and I'll have my secretary put you straight through. Oh, and Robert, get the bastard."

"I will, Linda."

Moore was deep in thought when Mary Ann walked in with a pad in her hand."Evans called. He will be here in twenty minutes with Jesse. And Evans intel checks out. I also checked her supervisor out. Not a very nice person. He's trying very hard to get rid of her. Rumor is he has a brother-in-law who needs a job. Robert, Jesse is good, damn good, and we need her."

"What about the trouble at the university?"

"The report said Jesse was set up. She supposedly broke into the university mainframe, specifically the science computer, and stole a bunch of plans. The university asked her to leave until the investigation was over. So, instead of waiting, she went out and hired the two most highly qualified computer experts. They not only proved her innocence, but got evidence showing it was her ex-fiancé and two of his friends. She got her degree, but it looks like the two families were not happy about this. They came down hard on her family. So, daddy said she disgraced the family, especially him, and would not let her come back on the property to get her belongings. Little brother stepped in and helped her get her own place. With his help she got this job here, if you want to call it that."

Moore leaned back in his chair."Bad about her family, but we need this young woman to work for us. Can Jesse pass our background check?"

"Oh, yes," answered Mary Ann.

"Good. When Jesse gets here, I want her on that chip as soon as possible and if the information is good, we going moving on it. Have Lieutenant Angles and Evans get Alpha and Bravo team ready. Have an extra medic attached to both teams. Alpha will be lead team going in, and all weapons will be on setting three. I don't know why, but I have a good feeling that chip will have the victim location and I want to go as soon as we get it."

"Yes, sir." She left the room.

No sooner did Mary Ann leave his office, a call came through. Moore saw Brigadier General Thomas Chayton's image.

"Well, I had to talk to him sooner or later. It might as well be now. Answer."

General Chayton appeared, red faced and tight lipped.

Oh, this isn't going to be good, Moore thought."Colonel Moore speaking. How may I help the General today?"

"Colonel. I'll get to the damn point. My contacts are telling me that certain people are getting classified information. Is that right, Colonel?"

"Yes, sir, I hate to say it's the truth. Linda Hardcastle told me her boss has the same report that I gave her only an hour ago," Moore replied.

"Not good, Colonel. Any idea how they're getting that information from a so-called secured system?"

"No, sir, the only one authorized here is the computer lab and the people that I have now are good, but not for this. A security checks will be made on all personnel, civilians, and military."

"You do that, Colonel. I didn't like that damn idea to switch data security to the computer lab, but I was overridden on it. Is that all?"

"Sir, we got a lead on the kidnapping case and, if the information is good, we will act on it immediately."

"And where did you get this information, Colonel?" Ask the General.

"It was sent to Sergeant Major Lincoln, sir. I have a specialist coming in now to verify it. I should know by tonight. The General will get a full report on a secure data line."

"All right, Colonel. I'll let you get to work and I'll be looking for your report. Keep on your guard. I don't like what's going on up there. Chayton out."

Moore reached over and tapped his keyboard."Call Gunny Sergeant Taylor."

After three rings, Gunny Taylor's face appeared. Taylor was in his fifties, short, pepper gray hair, brown eyes, and a jagged scar running from his temple to his jaw line.

"Gunny Taylor speaking. How can I help you, Colonel?" he said.

"Gunny, did you get the word?" Moore said.

"Yes, sir. Alpha and Bravo are geared up as we speak, sir, and an extra medic has been added to both teams."

"Outstanding, Gunny. Send my weapon up to me and let the team leaders know I will be going with them."

"Yes, sir. I'll have one of my people bring your weapon to you. Anything else that I can do for you, sir?"

"Yes, Gunny, alert Charlie and Delta, I want them on standby. Right now everything is not going too well and I don't want anything to come back and bite us in the butt. It never hurts to be prepared."

"Roger that, sir. Everything will be ready for you, Colonel."

"Thanks, Gunny. Moore out."

Moore was walking around his desk when the office door opened. Lieutenant Evans and Mary Ann walked in with a young woman.

"Colonel, I would like you to meet Jessie. Jessie, this is Colonel Robert Moore, Head of Security."

Moore studied her for a minute, a tall, young woman with black shoulder length hair. Yet, the most remarkable feature was her beautiful green eyes. At first glance, they glowed like green emerald."A very beautiful young lady and five degrees, not bad," he thought.

"Miss Hitoml Ayano, it's a pleasure to meet you,"he said, seeing surprise and then a smile that lit up her face.

"Thank you, Colonel. It's nice to meet you, too. I'm surprised you pronounced my name correctly. Not many people can," Jesse said.

Moore smiled at her."I can see why you were given Hitoml. If I'm not mistaken, it means"woman with beautiful eyes" and it suits you very well." Again, the surprise appeared on her face and her smile grew even brighter.

"Oh, trying to be a charmer, huh? I'd better keep my eye on you. So, Evans says you have a problem. What can I do for you Colonel?" she said.

"Sir, with your permission?" asked Evans.

"Dismissed, Lieutenant, and thank you," answered Moore.

Evans left the office with a phone in hand.

"Jessie, everything I tell you in this office stays in this office. You're not to discuss this with anybody. Do you understand me?"

Jessie answered,"Yes, Colonel, I understand you completely. You have my word."

"Good." Moore told her how Mary Ann found the note and chip on her desk while he was in his office and never knew anybody was in the outer office."I want to know how they got into this building and if the chip is clean. Can you do that, Jessie?"

Jessie had a little smile."Today is your lucky day. I have two programs. One is for little surprises and the other one is for people who come in without permission. Now, if you would show me where I can set my equipment up, I will get right on it, Colonel."

Moore motioned with his hand towards his desk."You can use my computer."

"Thank you, Colonel." Jessie walked over to the computer and set her backpack down. She quickly brought out a laptop and computer pad and started hooking everything up."Colonel, I modified this computer pad to run a series for viruses and other bad things. I also hooked up my laptop so I could moderate it. So, if it does have viruses on it, it stays on my laptop. Okay, Colonel, can I have the chip and we can see what is on it?"

Moore handed Jessie the chip and she put it in the computer pad. The screen lit up:"VIRUS SCREEN READY." She hit enter and the scan started. Jessie turned to Moore and Mary Ann."This should take one or two hours depending on if we have no problems. Also, you wanted to know who's been making little visits at night. That might take a while."

Moore's eyes got a little bigger and a smile appeared."One or two hours? Ha, it usually takes longer than that."

Jessie smiled."That's why I get the big bucks, Colonel."

Mary Ann started laughing."Oh, yes, I do like this young lady. Reminds me of myself when I was her age."

So, you have a program for the security cameras and locks?"

"Yes, Colonel. But, I need your computer terminals for that and I give you my word that I will not put any virus, back door, or command codes in your system. So, please have one of your people check out my work anytime you like. You won't hurt my feelings."

"I appreciate that, please, continue."

"Here goes, Colonel." Jessie brought out a small box from her backpack. She opened it to reveal cards with chips. Jessie found what she wanted and turned back to Moore and Mary Ann.

"If you please, could you bring up your system and we'll see who's been leaving you the little presents."

Mary Ann entered her code."All yours, Jessie."

"Thank you, Sergeant Major Lincoln?"

"You can call me Mary Ann."

"Thank you. This will look for back doors, viruses, or codes that will let anybody in your system." The computer beeped and showed an illegal program was in the system."Do you wish it to continue?"

Mary Ann entered her code and it beeped twice to show the program in progress. Jessie studied the screen for a few seconds. Satisfied everything was good, she was about to speak when her laptop sounded like glass breaking."Damn, that was fast." She watched the data grow as Moore and Mary Ann stepped up behind her to see the screen.

"Wow, talk about good karma. Colonel, the data is good. No bugs, viruses, and no backdoor. I can put your people at the front door where the kidnapper is hiding. This is freaky. Colonel, it shows the location of two cameras. They have two escape routes, one outside and one inside. It even shows the override codes to open the door. Whoever sent this to you wants this person caught very bad."

"And I want that bastard just as bad. Jessie, that information will save the young lady who was kidnapped last night. I don't care how I get him, as long as I find that young lady."

Jessie felt a cold chill run down her spine."Damn, you have him, Colonel. Mary Ann, I need your code so I can send you the information." Jessie watched the screen as the information came up."Sending it to you now."

"I have it and sending it to Lieutenant Evans and Angles. They have it and will be ready to go when the Colonel arrives."

"Good, let Evans know I will be there in fifteen."

Moore turned to go when a knock at the door stopped

him.''Enter,'' Moore said. A young private came in.

"Sir, Private King reporting as ordered, sir."

Moore saw the private go to a rigid attention. Perspiration trailed down the side of his head as his face turned pale. *Lord, the kid is scared to death. He must be from the bunch that got here last week*, he thought.

"Thank you, private, just set the case on the table and I'll sign the clipboard for you," Moore said.

"Yes, sir." Case on the table, King turned and handed the clipboard to Moore.

As Moore signed, he asked,''How do you like being stationed on the moon?''

King was startled by the question, but his face lit up.''I never thought I would be chosen to be here, sir.''

Moore smiled back.''I know what you mean. I was surprised, too, when my orders came for the moon.'' He handed the clipboard back.''Keep up the good work, King.''

"Thank you, sir. I will." King marched out the door more confident.

Jessie looked to Moore.''That was very nice, Colonel. I thought he was going to pass out for a minute there.''

"I took his mind off of it. Now, I have a young trooper with confidence. If you ladies will excuse me." Case in hand, Moore headed to his inner office.

Moore set the case on a smaller desk, and took out the S.G.R-four handgun and three ammo clips. All three clips had a green light, meaning they were charged. Satisfied his weapon and clips were in working order, he went to his closet and opened the double doors. On the right side were extra uniforms and shoes and on the left his battle armor. He took his body suit from the hanger and turned to his bed and laid it out. Quickly, he stripped down and put on the body suit. Sliding his hands down the sleeves into the gloves, he worked his fingers into each slow. Moving back to his closet, Moore quickly put on the rest of his armor. Sitting his helmet on the desk, Moore picked up his weapon and one clip. He slid the clip into the handle and heard a metallic click and felt a slight vibration. He looked where the rear sight used to be. Now a small screen comes on, showing him that the weapon is charged with twenty-four shots. Moore slipped his handgun into the holster, and then put the two clips in their slots beside the handgun. As he put on his helmet, he touched a small switch on the right side. The visor slid into place and a screen showed all seals were good. The battery and air were at one hundred percent. The unit was good for twenty-four hours. He touched the helmet again and the screen showed the helmet was unlocked and the visor slid up. Taking his helmet off, he moved back to the outer office.

Hearing the door open, Jessie turned as Moore walked out in his battle suit."Damn, I would like to have one of those, Colonel. That is totally rad."

Moore smiled."Well, maybe we can get you one, Jessie. Before I leave, do you have anything to secure our com system? I don't trust what we have and I need it secure for only my people."

"Already on it. Mary Ann told me about your problem before she left for the office, and I downloaded a program for it. But, this will only be good on two or three lines. Anything else will take longer, and don't worry, Colonel, nobody will have access but you and your people. I guarantee it."

"Thanks, Jessie. You have done an outstanding job for us and I am very grateful. I will personally put a commendation in your files. You more than earned it."

Mary Ann strode back in the office mumbling to herself and stopped in front of Jessie."Sugar, I am so sorry. I just finished talking with your boss and he fired you and put in the paperwork so you will be on the next flight back to Earth. I tried to talk to him, but the bastard hung up on me. Colonel, permission to go to the little bastard's office."

"Permission denied, Sergeant Major. We have more important things to do here. Do you understand?"

Mary Ann snapped to attention and shouted."I understand the Colonel. I will not be visiting the little bastard's office today."

"Very good. Jessie, I'm sorry about this. I didn't mean for you to lose your job. I will personally call your boss back and explain it to him."

"Don't worry about it Colonel. It's no big surprise; he was not happy with me when I outdid his wife brother, and he let me know about it every day. You probably won't like this, but I need a job, I'm good at what I do, and if you ran a security check, you know what degrees I have. I really don't want to go back to Earth, so please consider my request. That's all I ask."

Keeping the surprise off his face, Moore studies Jessie for a second or two."All right, this is what we will do. Mary Ann will supervise you. If anything comes up, she will brief you on it. I need you to keep working on the chip and our other problem. Will this be good for you?"

"Thank you, Colonel, that's more than generous. I will not let you down, that I promise you."

"And I will hold you to that. Mary Ann, I leave her with you. Ladies." He turned and left his office already concentrating on his next problem.

Jessie watched Moore leave the office and shook her head. *I don't want that man after me*, she thought.

Turning to Mary Ann,"All right, let's get this assholes," she said to Mary Ann. Her laptop beeped twice and as she studied the screen. Her eyes got bigger."No freaking way."

"What's wrong, Jessie?" Mary Ann said.

"You are not going to believe this, but there's more information on this chip and the Colonel will want to know about it."

***

Moore stepped out of the elevator into a warm wind of activity around him. He stops and studies the scene. The sergeants were getting their people together to be loaded in the first two trucks and the last of the supply was loaded on the third truck. The two medical units was loaded and the medical sergeant had his people in formation waiting for orders. Satisfied, Moore made his way over to the armory, where he saw a gunny sergeant who was in charge of the armory. Gunny sergeant Nick Taylor noticed Moore and handed the clipboard back to the corporal.

"That's good, Jennings, carry on with it," he said.

He turned to Moore."Everything is ready to go, Colonel. I took the liberty of adding two emergency vehicles to the convoy. I brought up the young troopers and broke them down into squads of four, each with a senior sergeant. They have been deployed to all entrances that go to the lower levels. We don't need civilians while this operation is ongoing."

"Good work, Gunny. Is there anything else I need to know?"

asked Moore.

"Yes, sir. Sergeant Major called, said someone named Jessie found more information on the chip and is working on it."

"Did the Sergeant Major say what it was?"

"Just you're not going to like it, sir."

"Damn. Okay, we deal with that when it comes. Let's get this show on the road, Gunny."

"All right, people!" shouted Gunny."Listen up. All personnel load up. Repeat, all personnel load up in your assigned trucks. Let's move it, people, we're leaving in five. Move it, move it, people!"

Moore moved to the front of the convoy where his Humvee and driver, Haley, were waiting.

"Morning, Colonel. Command said we have three secured lines now. Is there anything else, sir?" said Haley.

"I'm good to go. Now, let's get this bastard." Putting on his helmet, Moore slid into his Humvee.

"Attention, all vehicles. We're moving out. Repeat, we're moving out."

The convoy moved towards the master elevator that will take them down to level nine. Moore's Humvee stopped in the center of the elevator. The two troop trucks moved on either side of the Humvee and the supply truck move up behind them. The two medical units stopped behind the troop trucks. Haley looked in her side mirrors and saw the other three trucks move up behind her.

"Is everybody in?" she asked over the radio. Getting a yes, she reached to a keypad and pushed close. The doors closed behind them and she tapped level nine. The elevator started to descend.

The doors opened on level nine and the convoy moved out on to a wide, two-lane road. They came upon a sign that says"Welcome to Tucker Hill." As they moved past that sign, they approached another that showed the sports complex to the left and the park and swimming pool to the right. They moved straight to town, took a left on Industrial Street, and continue into town. It was reminiscent of a small town on Earth, but instead of houses, there are only apartments. There are also office buildings, stores, markets, a church and schools; everything for the families who will live here. The town was still in night mode, but in forty-five minutes the lights would come up like a sunrise and go through a full day, until sunset.

Haley glanced at the GPS."Colonel, coming up to the security substation."

"Thank you," answered Moore.

"Attention, trucks three, four and five, move out as planned to the substation," said Haley.

"Roger that. Substation will be up in twenty minutes," answered Lieutenant Harper.

Five minutes later, Haley announced their arrival."Attention, convoy, we're coming up to our stop. Bravo team, deploy and move to take up position behind the target warehouse. Signal when you're in position."

"Roger that. Bravo one, out."

The Humvee and two trucks turn into a parking lot two buildings down from their target.

Moore get out of his Humvee and moves to the front to watch the Troopers unload. He watched while Bravo company disappeared down the alley and Alpha leader gave her final instructions. He turns and looked to the target warehouse."I have you now."

"Sir, Bravo in position," announced Alpha Leader.

He looked around him, all ready to go, just waiting for the word."Get it done, lieutenant," answered Moore.

"Alpha, go."

Alpha rushed the warehouse. One trooper stopped and raised his weapon to his shoulder. He lines his red dot with the first security camera and fires. There was an odd sound and sparks flew. The second camera went like the first, in a shower sparks.

"Cameras are down," the shooter announced.

Another trooper got to the door with four troopers for cover, their weapons pointed to the doors. Pad in hand, he plugged it into the security panel and punched in the code. He waited a few seconds, got a beep, and entered the final code. The light turned from red to green.

"Go!" he shouts.

The two nearest troopers push the doors open and put wedges underneath them, delivering a quick kick to secure them in place. They move through the doors, breaking into tiers of four and moving from room to room, calling out clear after close inspection.

Moore and Haley entered the warehouse with Haley in front, weapon up. They followed the troopers down the hall when a signal was given and everybody come to a halt.

"Alpha Leader, we have a door slightly open with lights on and I hear movement," said a trooper.

"Is it our target or the girl?" asked Alpha Leader.

"Don't know. Don't want to move the door. He might see it or hear it."

"Roger that. Have your people on either side of the door with flashbangs at the ready and, if you see the target, take him down. The girl is our main concern, so protect her at all costs. Let me know when you're ready."

"Roger that, LT."

The Troopers moved on either side of the door with flash bangs and weapons ready. Alpha leader got green lights on her visor.

She took a deep breath."Go."

The door flies open and four flashbangs go in. Three seconds later, four big bangs of blinding light. They rushed in left and right. Nobody was there and all the furniture was scattered towards the left wall. A door was in the back. They spread out when someone called out over the radio,"I found the girl. She's on a table near the right wall." Then all that could be heard was him throwing up. He took off his helmet, then quiet.

A new voice calls out,"Oh, Sweet Mother. Medic, medic! I need a medic! Jenny, get your ass over here. Damn, he cut her open, man. He cut her from her neck to her crotch, man. Somebody help me to stop this bleeding. There's so much blood. It's everywhere, Jenny, you can see her insides. Oh, God, Jenny." His voice got louder with panic."I think she's coming around; I can hear her moan and her eyes are starting to open, hurry!"

"Okay, calm down, I'm here. When he sees what's on the table he mumbles a prayer. Father in Heaven, help me save this woman. Sasha, I need you over here, now. It's going to take two of us, and call for a trauma team and doctor to get here stat. They need to bring all the blood they can. Make sure you tell them to get surgery ready. If she lives long enough," he said.

In any operation, there is only one rule: finish securing the area. But when they heard the trooper crying out they turned to see what was wrong. They saw only a body covered with blood, one arm dangling from the table as blood dripped from her fingertips, making a puddle on the floor. Only one young trooper stood staring through a door to total darkness and to a hallway that lead to other rooms. The trooper thought she saw movement, but was not sure. A friend called to her and she turned her head. In that instant, she saw movement in the corner of her eye and knew she had made a very a bad mistake.

A dark figure stood very still in the dark, his weapon close to his chest and another hanging from his shoulder. He watched as the trooper stared at him and he thought, *you can't see me, can you? No, you can't, ha, ha, ha. That's why they sent me to the moon, yes. To find the truth and I did, because I saw you take some of us. Ha, ha, ha, ha, you thought nobody saw you, but I did. I know your secret, oh, yes I do. Ha, ha, ha, but I need proof to tell the world, so I captured two of your males for information, but they wouldn't talk. No, they would rather die than talk, so I took one of your females and here you are. Ha, ha, ha.*

The trooper's head turned and he started moving as he brought his weapon to his shoulder.

He laughed maniacally,"you have made a very bad mistake."

The first round took the trooper down, catching everybody by surprise. His madman laugh was even louder. His first weapon locked back, empty. Dropping it, he brought his second weapon up with his right hand, and his left hand brings out a flashbang.

He backs through the door and shouts,"It's time to play hide and seek!" He disappears in to the blackness, only leaving the echo of a madman's laugh through the hallway and room.

Moore moved to the door when an AK Forty-Seven opened fire. Haley hit him with her full weight and knocked him down to the floor. Bullets went through the wall where he was standing just seconds ago.

Getting off of him, Haley asked,"Sir, are you alright?"

She moved to the opposite wall, weapon aimed at the door."I'm fine, Corporal." Another flashbang goes off, followed by laughter and then silence.

"Sweet Jesus, Colonel, did you hear that bastard? He's crazy," said Haley.

"Yes, I heard him, Haley. This has just gotten worse. He has to be brought down fast. No telling what he might do." They heard cries for medics as people got over the shock. Moore motioned to Haley to get up so he could see the damage.

"All right, people, let's get our wounded tended to. I want four people to search that room. I want to know where he got out. Watch for booby traps. Alpha to Bravo."

"Go, Alpha."

"Bravo, our little rat got out somewhere. Don't know is he coming to you or not."

"Roger that. We will keep an eye out. Do you need another medic, Alpha?"

"Negative. The trucks are coming. Alpha out."

Haley moved closer to the door, looked in and yelled"Clear!"

A moment later, she hears"clear" echo back.

"Okay, Colonel, go ahead." She stepped over to one side for Moore to enter the room.

Locating the wounded, Moore moved to them.

The medic looked up and said,"Can I help you, sir?"

"How bad is it, Miller?"

"One critical, one leg wound, and three slightly wounded. The slightly will be back on duty. The rest will be transferred back to the substation, sir."

"Good, and their names?"

"Private John Huston and Specialist Donny White, sir."

"And the young lady?"

"Sorry, sir, I don't know."

"No, no, don't be, Miller. You're doing a good job. I can find out. Thank you and carry on."

Moore and Haley went over to where the girl was. Lieutenant Angles glanced up and saw them coming.

"Sir."

"Lieutenant. How's the girl?"

"Jimmy and Sasha are working on her now. A trauma team will be here in five. It's bad, Colonel. I'm amazed she's still alive." Pausing for a second,"Sir, I take full responsibility for this. I should have come in a little more cautious. Instead, I just bulldozed through here and had five of my people hurt. Sorry, sir."

"Hell, lieutenant, you did it by the book. That's all I ask. When this doesn't bother you, that's when you need to step away from it." Moore set a hand on her shoulder."Now, Eve, where did that little bastard get off to?"

That caught her by surprise and a smile spread on her face."I better find out, one moment, please, sir." She turned and shouted,"Sergeant White, Sergeant Davis, I want to know how that little bastard got out. I want answers now."

Moore was watching his lieutenant when Haley said,"Sir, medical are here."

He turned to see four corpsman with gurneys. Two went right to where the girl was and two more headed straight for the wounded troopers. Moore glanced back to see the head doctor, Major Mary Carmichael, talking to one of her staff. She looked to Moore and nodded as she rushed over to where the girl was being loaded on the gurney.

"Haley, you know you have a good command when your people know their jobs."

"Yes, sir."

"Lead One for Alpha Leader."

"Go, Alpha."

"Sir, my troopers found where he got out and his command center. There are enough weapons and supplies here to last a month. They also have a computer and laptop. We need an expert for them. Also, the two missing males are in another room and it looks bad, but you're not going to believe this, sir, but we have three more in a back room and they're alive."

"You have three and they're alive?"

"Yes, sir. The medic said alive, but asleep."

"I'm on my way," he said as he went through the door and saw Angles by the last room.

"See for yourself," she said, motioning towards the open door.

Moore stepped in and saw two males and one female on old army camp beds covered with blankets. He walked between them, not believing they're alive.

He glanced to the medic,"Nothing is wrong. You sure?"

"Sure as I can be, sir. Seems like somebody just put them to sleep and they don't have a scratch on them."

"Colonel, how come he killed the males and tried for the girl, but not these three?" asked Angles.

Making his decision, he turns to Haley,"have everybody leave the room and guard the door, please."

"All right, everybody, you heard the Colonel. Let's go," said Haley.

After the room was empty, he said,"this goes no farther, Lieutenant, but these three here were taken by a different person. The woman and the two dead males were taken by that crazy bastard. Finding these three is a miracle in itself."

"Two? Two of them you said? Damn, this is bad. Colonel, if it's two of them now, how do we know if more are out there or not?"

"We don't, but we will assume there are. So, brief your sergeants, you can tell them there is more than one, but that's all. Understand, lieutenant."

"Yes ,sir, I understand completely."

"Good, dismissed, lieutenant," answer Moore.

He watched her leave and said,"Haley, contact the substation and tell them we found three civilians here, and have their identities verified. I also want a thorough medical exam done, and then contact command to send a forensic team and the detective down here. Oh, the morgue, too. I want two guards stationed here. You got all that?" asked Moore.

"Yes, sir, and Sergeant Major is on the line," she said and left the room.

"Sergeant Major, you called?" asked Moore.

"Colonel, I'm in the warehouse with Jessie. She has information you need to know," answered Mary Ann.

"Come straight to the back door, I will meet you there." Moore got there when Mary Ann and Jessie stepped in.

"All right, Sergeant Major, I know this is not going to be good. So, let's get it over with."

"Yes, sir. Jessie knows more about it. I'll let her tell you."

The visor came up and Jessie asked,"Can I take my helmet off, Colonel?"

"Go ahead. How do you like the combat suit?"

"I'm loving it. I hate to do this to you, but you have a terrorist, and the one you're after is Ronnie Rodriguez: thirty-five, black hair, brown eyes, citizen of Mexico, and one of the worst. The last time anybody has seen him was a year ago. Mr. Rodriguez had a falling out with his cell. They didn't care how bad he mutilated their enemies, but when he started doing it to his own people, they got scared and decided it was time to get rid of him. So, the safe house he was in blew up and all they found of him was a finger. From what I can tell, he's been here for two months now. Counting Rodriguez, the chip says there are six infiltrators. Four in maintenance, including Rodriguez. I think we found our leak, because this one works in the computer lab; no name on him yet but hopefully soon, Colonel. The sixth one is female, a Miss Sandhill, forty, mousy brown hair, blue eyes, and she's English. Sorry, Colonel, it look like she's the secretary for Mrs. Hardcastle, the base manager. Colonel, I know what their mission is and it's not good."

Moore looked at Jessie in stunned silence."How do you know all this and where did you get it from?"

For the first time, Jessie looked anxious, as she looks at the people nearby.

Mary Ann stepped up and touched her shoulder."Don't worry, I'll make this easy for you. Listen up, everybody. As of now, this is classified information. You're not allowed to talk to anybody, do I make myself clear?" Getting a unanimous"yes ma'am," she gestured for Jessie to continue.

"The information came from the chip your friends left you. Colonel, the target is the cold fusion plant here. I have the warehouse, and how they're going to deliver the bomb to it. Hell, Colonel, I have all their plans."

Still stunned, Moore asks,"You have their plans and it was on the chip? Is that what I heard?"

"Yes, sir, you did. I told you they really wanted you to catch these guys."

"Damn, this changes everything. Jessie, there's a laptop and a computer here. I need you to do your magic and do it fast. Someone show her where it is, please," said Moore.

A trooper steps up, and said,"This way, please, ma'am."

"Sergeant Major, call in all personnel and have Sun take charge of Charlie and Delta. I want them down here now. Moore to Command."

"Command, Lieutenant Bishop here."

"Lieutenant, we're going into a terrorist alert; this is not a drill. Have security lockdown the reactor room exit. No one goes in or out. I want four snipers. Send two to Evans and two to Angles. Be advised there's more than one terrorist. Three others will probably meet up with the one we're chasing. They have automatic weapons and explosives. Alert medical at substation nine it's going to get bad. You get all that, lieutenant?"

"Yes, sir. My people are putting it out now. Will that be shoot on sight, sir?"

"Damn right it is. Nobody is to get to that warehouse but us."

"Sir, reactor room is secure. Command out."

Mary Ann walked over to Moore."The Computer lab guy is William W Scott, forty, black hair, brown eyes. He is head of security for computers there and it looks like he is at home."

"Mary Ann, I leave this in your hands. I want one of them alive and I don't care which one."

"Don't worry, Colonel. I will have Gunny Taylor go for Scott and I will go get Sandhill, piece of cake."

"And how are you going to do that, Mary Ann?" Moore asked suspiciously.

Giving him an evil grin,"Why, I'm going to go in there and stun the bitch, sir."

"Mary Ann, you can't." He stopped and shook his head,"Linda has been good to us and I hate to have her mad at us."

"Don't worry, sir, your girlfriend will be safe with me."

"Watch yourself, Sergeant Major."

"I'm sorry, won't happen again and don't worry, sir, she has one of the communicators for emergencies just like this. I will give her a call and let her know what's going on. She'll be fine, sir."

Haley stepped in and said,"Sir. Jessie just sent the address for the warehouse and an overhead view of the area, and, I don't believe this, but also where booby traps are set up and where caches of weapons are available. Damn, talk about good."

"Lieutenant,"Moore shouted."Load them up, we have a terrorist to hunt down."

Jessie walked out in time to hear Haley say,"Colonel, put your helmet on, please."

"Are we ready to go?" Jessie asked.

"Yes, we are. Did you get everything you needed?" asked Mary Ann.

"Oh, yes. I got everything and if we're going after Sandhill, I need her computer for twenty minutes and I'll give you the location to her boss," Jessie said.

"Is that so? This just gets better and better," answered Mary Ann.

A trooper came up to them, her faceplate open to show a pretty young woman with freckles over her nose, and grey eyes.

"Betty, did you get it?" asked Mary Ann.

Betty handed her a syringe."This will put her down for twelve hours, Sergeant Major," she said with a smile.

She took it and said,"Outstanding. Where's Susan?"

Another trooper stepped around the corner; her faceplate was up. You could see strands of blonde hair around her face, and brown eyes. She said in a thick, Texas drawl,"I'm right here, Sergeant Major."

"All right, ladies, let's go. We have a terrorist to catch."

***

The elevator opened on level ten to reveal a convoy. The Humvee left to follow the two troop trucks. Captain Sun read the information on her pad and looked to her driver.

"This is a lot of information here, Davis," she said.

"Yes, Ma'am. It's more then we usually get. I can't believe we got their name and location of the warehouse," he said

"You got that straight. How did they get all this information? I mean—" that's when the rocket slammed into the back of the Humvee and flipped it over on its side. The second rocket barely missed them and hit the building behind them.

Davis looked around, disoriented for a moment. Then, he realized they were on their side. Hanging by his safety restraints, Davis starts moving his arms and legs for broken bones or open wounds. Satisfied, he looked down to Sun and asks,"Captain, are you okay?"

"Yeah, just shook up a bit. Nothing's broken. Do you see any bleeding anywhere?" Sun said.

"No, ma'am, you look good. Damn. What the hell hit us, a missile?" he said.

"No, if it was a missile we wouldn't be talking."

"Damn. Don't those bastards know we on a space station?

They can die, too."

"I don't think they really care and we're lucky they used old law rockets that were used on personnel, Humvee and troop trucks."

"Well, that's good to know, but let's get the hell out of here before they get it right."

They heard yelling over the comm system. A trooper shouted,"There! He's in the alley; lay down cover fire. You two, get the captain and corporal out."

Davis grabbed the steering wheel in his left hand as he hit the quick release on his harness. He saw that Sun was having trouble with her release, so he lowered himself to her.

"Don't worry, Captain I have this," he said.

Two Troopers came around to the windshield and one said,"Turn away." When they did, the troopers broke out the rest of it. They helped Sun out as Davis grabbed their weapons and handed them out.

As he crawled out he asked,"Where is that son of a bitch at?" He eased to the front and looked up in time to see an AK Forty-Seven appear around the corner and fire back down the alley.

"There you are," Davis said. He held his weapon out to Sun."Will you hold my weapon for me, Captain?"

As she took it she asked,"What are you going to do, corporal?"

"I'm going to blow his little ass out in front for us," answered Davis.

"Get it done," said Sun, a little irritated.

"Yes ma'am. Watch and learn private. Covering fire," he shouted.

He stepped out from the Humvee and threw the grenade. It went high up and hit the corner in an angle, then bounced to hit the back wall and land behind the terrorist. The grenade went off and a terrorist landed in the middle of the alley. There was silence, when the private behind Davis said in amazement,"No freaking—"

A second and bigger explosion caught everybody completely by surprise. Some troopers that were near the body did not survive, while others were knocked down and the ones left standing looked around in stunned silence.

"What the frack just happen? Terry, Terry where are you? You were just here. Tom. have you seen Terry? Tom, Tom," someone says."What the frack happened?" He falls to his knees, holding himself and rocking back and forth. Moans and cries for help could be heard as people snapped out of their shock.

Standing up on shaky legs, Sun looked around and stumbled to the Humvee, not believing her eyes.

In a shaky voice she calls out."All right people listen up." Nobody could hear her; too much shouting and screaming. *No*, she thinks. *I have to make them hear me.* She takes several steps away from the Humvee and screams."I said 'listen up, people.'" Everybody stopped and looked to her."All right, lieutenants, get your people to spread out and help the wounded. Medic, find a place to set up for the wounded. A call will be put in for more help and I need three people to go in the alley to see what else he had in there. Okay, people, do your jobs."

Lying on his back, Davis started to move, and slowly he sat up. He put two hands on his helmet and said,"Man, this is not good, not good at all." He rolled over to his left and put his hand on the ground, but he felt something else. He looked. A leg. He mumbles and follows the leg up to the owner.

"Surprise," he said."All hell, not you." It was the private that told him he couldn't bounce the grenade off the wall. He was lying there with a perfect round hole in his visor. Davis looked away."I'm sorry, man. I didn't know he was a suicide bomber. Please, forgive me."

Sun watches her people for a few seconds more. Satisfied everything was under control, she turned to locate her corporal and saw him leaning over a trooper. She hurried over to him and kneeled onto one knee and put a hand on his shoulder.

"Davis, are you all right?" she said.

"I'm all right, ma'am, but this is not good. First, we're looking for a kidnapping and now we have terrorist. Not to mention that he had a suicide vest on. If he had one, you can be sure the others will too. And to top it off, we don't even know what kind of equipment they have. Ma'am, this is going to get a lot worse before it gets better," he said, taking his helmet off.

"I know, but we have a job to do, so contact the medical division to have emergency teams sent here for our MIA and casualties. Then, call the Colonel and bring him up to speed. Let them know we're still on mission. Get it done, Corporal," Sun said.

"Roger that, ma'am. Medic One, this is Four, Medic One, this is Four. Come in, please," Davis said.

"This is Medic One, go Four," Medic One responded.

"Medic One, be advised we have MIA and casualties. The LZ is secured for now, but be advised that may change. I'm sending the location to you now," said Davis.

"Have location now, sending emergency units out, Four. Can you tell me any details, Four?" said Medic One.

A suicide bomber caught us by surprise, and it's bad."

"Roger that, Four, we will be ready. Medical One out."

"Davis to Haley, come in."

"Haley here, go, Davis."

"Be advised, Charlie and Delta were in an ambush. Command vehicle is out of commission. We have MIA and casualties. Emergency personnel are on their way. Terrorist is dead, but was wearing suicide bomb vest and if he was wearing one, you can bet the others will be, too. These bastards are going to cause as much damage as they can, Haley," Davis said.

"Damn, we heard the explosion over here. Are you able to stay on mission and do you have count? You know the old man will want to know," Haley said.

"Negative on count, will let you know, and yes, we're still on mission. Be advised, the emergency vehicles are on site now," said Davis.

"Roger that. Be waiting for your report. Haley out."

As he turned back, he heard a trooper report in."Captain, you are not going to believe this. You need to get over here now, ma'am."

"I'm on my way," said Sun.

Sun and Davis trot over to the alley where the other three troopers went. She stepped around the corner and was stunned at what she saw. Taking off her helmet, she stood there and stared at the assault rifles, animal, grenades, satchel bombs and four law rockets. Her face went pale and she got a cold shiver run down her back. She looked at Davis.

"If you didn't take down that terrorist, this would have been a lot worse, Davis, she said. He was about to say something, when she raised her hand."No. Enough said."

"Yes, Ma'am," Davis said.

"Ma'am I have already called a truck to load all this up. We can't afford to leave this here," sad Lieutenant Baldacci.

"Excellent, Lieutenant. I leave it to you. But hurry it up, were still on mission," said Sun.

"Roger that," answered Baldacci.

A trooper, a woman with blonde hair and piercing blue eyes, hurries up to Sun."Ma'am, Sergeant Acord reporting."

"Let's hear it, Sergeant," answers Sun.

"Ma'am, there are eight dead and Lieutenant Travis of Charlie company is one. Fifteen are critical and five wounded. The medical crew has informed me that the hospital has been open and our people are heading there as we speak," said Acord in a hard voice.

"Damn. All right, Sergeant, Charlie Company is yours now. Take good of it. We paid a heavy price and this will not happen again. Form up and check all gear for damages. I want scouts sent out. Have everybody load up. We're going to do this by the book," said Sun.

They all shouted,"Roger that, ma'am!" and went off to do their jobs. She turn to tell Davis to contact the Colonel, but stopped when she saw the shocked look on his face.

"Davis?" she asked, concerned. Then she hears it, too."Mortar."

Davis looks from Sun to the explosions six blocks to the north."How the hell did they get this equipment up here," he screams.

"This is bad. They're hitting the area where the Colonel is," said Sun.

"Captain, we need to do something. Those mortars will tear this area up and nobody will be able to live here. Not to mention the level beneath us."

"All personnel to the trucks, repeat, all personnel to the trucks. Scouts go to the sports complex, especially the soccer fields. That's the only open areas to put us at a disadvantage and a clear field of fire for mortars. Do not make contact. I want to know how many there are and what kind of equipment they have. Davis, contact the Colonel and tell him we know where the mortars are," Sun said.

"Roger that, Captain," answered Davis.

***

**

"Colonel, Davis just called. They were ambushed and have heavy casualties. The terrorist is dead, but he was wearing a suicide vest. Emergency units are there and they're still good to go for the mission," said Haley.

This news stunned Moore, his rage building slowly. He turned to Haley with a red face and thin lips."How the hell did they know to set up a ambush there? Okay, spread the word around that these bastards are wearing suicide vests. I specifically want snipers, team of two, with the four companies. They are to shoot on sight. Do you have that, Haley?" said Moore.

"Roger that," Haley said. She paused with a funny look which turned to fear."We've got to go. Move, sir, move. Incoming, Incoming!"

Time slows down. Haley looked over her shoulder to see four troopers that didn't move fast enough. The first mortar hit in front of them with a brilliant flash of light, the shockwave almost knocking them down. Two more troopers were caught by the second blast. One skidded across the road, but the second one slammed into the back of a troop truck and slid down in a crumpled heap.

"Haley, Haley left!" screams Moore.

The shock wave lifted them off their feet and flung them in to the alley.

***

Mary Ann and Jessie stepped off the elevator with two troopers and moved down the hall to the manager's office.

"Ladies, when we enter the office, Betty and Susan will break off to the other side of the door and watch me. Jessie, when I give the word, you go to her desk and start your search," said Mary Ann."I will walk to Hardcastle's door, demanding to see her. Hopefully that should catch her off guard. When she sees I'm still advancing to the inner office door, she will jump up to block my way. That's when I'll nail her sorry ass. Any questions?"

"No, ma'am," they said.

"Good, we're here."

They stopped in front of the manager's office. Mary Ann took her helmet off and put it underneath her left arm. She checked her handgun to make sure it would come out of the holster smoothly. Taking a deep breath, she said,"Let's do this."

Mary Ann hurried through the door as the two troopers stepped to either side and Jessie followed four steps behind."Miss Sandhill, we have an urgent security matter, so I just stepped in to brief her. No need to get up."

"Finally," Sandhill said."No, wait, wait." Jumping up from her desk, she hurried over to the door."You can't just go in." She was stunned to see a weapon in Mary Ann hand. She looked at the weapon for a few seconds longer, then up to see an evil smile on the Sergeant Major's face.

"I have you now bitch," Mary Ann said in a low voice.

The stunned look went away and a killing fury burned in Sandhill's eyes. She screams as she leaped toward Mary Ann. Mary Ann fired with delight dancing in her eyes and that evil smile on her lips. Sandhill slammed in to the door and slid down with that image burn in her mind.

Mary Ann moved to her and going to one knee, syringe in hand. She glanced back to her two troopers.

"Susan, call for a medic and wait out in the hallway. No one is to interfere with them, got that," said Mary Ann.

"Yes, ma'am," replied Susan.

"Jessie, start your search," said Mary Ann.

"On it," said Jessie

"Betty, give me a hand, and we will put her on the floor over here," said Mary Ann. Picking up Sandhill's arm, she pushed her sleeve up to reveal a small knife."My, my, what nice toys she has. Make sure you search her real good."

"Damn, Sergeant Major, no telling what she has on her," said Betty.

"That's why we're going to do a full body scan when we get back to HQ. She's not going to commit suicide or go anywhere," said Mary Ann. Giving the injection, she stood up and moved back so Betty could search for more weapons. Putting the cap on the syringe, she stepped around and went to the door."Okay, Linda, come on out."

The door opened and Linda came out. She looked down at her

secretary, then back to Mary Ann."I hope to hell you know what you're doing. If you're wrong, this is going to get very bad and I can't help you anymore."

"Believe me, Linda, we are not wrong and you will have the evidence to back it up."

Jessie hurried over to the desk and pulled out the chair. Backpack on the chair, she takes out her laptop and hooks it to the computer. Starting her program, she watches for a few minutes as it breaks through the computer firewall. Satisfied, she turns her attention to the desk and starts searching the drawers. When she gets to the bottom right-hand drawer and pulls it open, she is stun for a few seconds, not believing what she sees. She jumps back, face pale.

"Oh damn. You need to see this, Mary Ann," says Jessie.

"What's wrong, Jessie?" says Mary Ann.

"I was searching Sandhill's desk and this is what I found," Jessie says, pointing down to the bottom right drawer.

"Bloody hell, is that what I think it is?" asks Linda.

"Oh, yeah, there's your proof: one bomber vest and a Glock. They must be ready to execute the plan. Betty, call the bomb squad and the detective," commands Mary Ann.

"Yes, ma'am," responds Betty.

"What else did you find, Jessie?" says Mary Ann.

Jessie was about to answer when her laptop sounded like broken glass. She stepped over and looked at the screen. She tapped a few keys and a smile spreads across her face.

"Our luck is still good; she was not in the office when the call came in. Everybody knew it but her, and when you came storming through that door, you caught her completely by surprise. Scored a big one for the good guys. I have the location where she sent all her information," says Jessie

"Wait a bloody minute. You mean you broke the encryption code and got the location?" says Linda.

"Yes, ma'am, I did," answered Jessie.

"Oh, that's right, you don't know. Linda, meet our new computer genius, Jessie. Jessie, Linda Hardcastle, the base manager here on the moon," said Mary Ann.

"Pleased to meet you and, yes, I have the location, but no name. I made two copies, one for you, Miss Hardcastle, and one for the Colonel," said Jessie.

"Good work. Anything else?" Ask Mary Ann.

"Oh yeah, she told them the project was ready and will wait for orders."

"Outstanding," Mary Ann answered."Betty, is everything ready at HQ?"

"Yes, ma'am. If she has anything else, we will find it," answered Batty.

"Good. Linda, if you to go to your computer and check to see if the copies are there, I'd appreciate it."

Linda hurried to her office and to her computer. Satisfied they were there, she hurried back."Yes, I do, and thanks for contacting me ahead of time. I appreciate it."

"Don't mention it. It's part of our service. All right, ladies, are you ready to go?" asked Mary Ann.

Putting her laptop in her backpack, Jessie fastened it and slung it over her shoulder."Yes ma'am."

The medical unit arrived and loaded up their prisoner.

"All right, let's go. We have a prisoner to get back to headquarters," declared Mary Ann.

Linda watched them leave and headed back to her office with a phone in her hand."Call Bruce Coleman."

Two rings,"Coleman here."

"Bruce, Linda. Come on up. You're my new secretary as of now," Linda said.

"I'm on my way," agreed Bruce.

She hung up and mumbled,"Bloody traitor."

***

The shock wave sent them flying into the alley. Hailey's training kicked in as she tucked into a roll to land on the balls of her feet and skidded to a stop. Moore didn't land too well. He collided with another trooper. His helmet came off and the troopers knee gave him a glancing blow to his head as he landed hard on the concrete, sliding into the other wall. Moore struggled to get up on his hands and knees, trying to get his breath.

Haley moved to him with his helmet and weapon."Colonel, your head is bleeding. Are you okay? Do you need a medic?"

"No, no. I'm fine. Let me get my breath," he said.

With Haley's help, Moore sat up against the wall and took a couple deep breaths. He reached up for his helmet.

"No, Colonel, you sit tight. You have a cut on the side of your head," she declared. Haley turned and yelled,"Medic! I need a medic here."

A medic got up from the trooper she was checking on and moved to them. Haley moved out of the way for the medic as she knelt down, taking her backpack off.

She looked over Moore carefully, stopping at the cut on his head."Colonel, do you remember who I am?" she asked.

He looked at her a few minutes."Yes, yes. You're Miller and you were at the warehouse."

She leaned back and held up her fingers."How many do you see, sir?" she said.

"Three," he answered.

"Good," she said."Do you have blurry vision?"

"No, but I do have one hell of a headache."

"I'll give you something for that, but first let me bandage your head." She reaches back in her medical bag and takes out a pair of latex gloves. With swift and confident hands, she cleans the blood with sterile wipes. A bandage with naproxen sodium covers the cut, held down by two strips of surgical tape. She gathers her trash and put it in a small bag. Then, she takes a water bottle from the side of the bag and hands it to Moore. As she takes out a pill bottle and opens it to shake out two capsules.

"Here you go, Colonel. This will not make you drowsy, but will take the pain away," said Miller.

Moore takes the two capsules and washes them down with water."Thank you," he said, returning the water bottle.

"You're welcome," Miller said, looking up at Haley."If he starts to get dizzy or throws up, let me know."

Before Moore said anything, somebody called for a medic. She nodded a goodbye and picked up her bag as she went to her next patient.

He watched her go and a smile spread on his face."She's a damn good trooper."

"Yes, she is." Haley said and handed him his helmet."Sir, you need to keep it more secure. It's not supposed to come off like this.

You could get hurt or die, and I can't have that."

"You know I don't like to wear this damn thing all the time, and you sound like the Sergeant Major," Moore rebuked.

"Thank you, sir. That's why she assigned me to you, to make sure you're safe. Now put on your helmet and keep it secure," said Haley.

"Damn, Corpus. you all think you can run this army these days. Lead One to Alpha Leader," mumbled Moore as he put his helmet on.

"Go lead," said Alpha Leader.

"Alpha, Charlie and Delta are handling this. Hold your position," said Moore.

"Will do sir."

"Haley, did you call for evac?" said Moore.

"Yes, sir and I also advised them the LZ is hot. Lieutenant Brave on the line," said Haley.

"Go Brave," said Moore.

"Colonel, we have the back secured. Two snipers are ready to go in. All they need is an open door," relayed Lieutenant Brave.

"Roger that. Contact J two on three. Door will open," said Moore.

"Contact J two on three. Brave out."

"Lead Two to One," said Lead Two.

"Go Two," said Moore.

"Sir. We're engaging the enemy now," said Lead Two.

Four small explosions could be heard and then two bigger explosions. Moore was almost knocked off his feet. It felt like a small earthquake. He felt the ground beneath his feet and his hand that was on the wall vibrated.

"Two. Are you trying to blow a hole through the damn floor?" asked Moore, regaining his balance.

"Couldn't be helped, sir. He had motion sensor machine guns. Had to use a law rocket, and like the first, he was wearing a vest. When he was hit, his vest went off, and mortars, too."

"All right, Two. Secure the area and get over here. One out," said Moore. He walked over to Haley."How is it out there?"

"Too quiet, Colonel, and I don't like it. There's two more. We don't know where they are and that scares me. This was planned for a long time and they knew what we would do," said Haley.

"I know. We've been caught flat-footed both times and I'll be damned if they get us this time," said Moore.

They heard a loud noise from across the street and the warehouse's front windows vibrated. The trooper's weapon covered the warehouse so the wounded could be moved. The noise got louder and louder as it got closer. Before they knew it, the windows and doors burst out, as a Humvee with two steel plates welded together in front came flying out of the building.

"Son of a bitch, when will I learn to keep my mouth shut. Not a word Haley, let's go!" yelled Moore.

The Humvee made it down the steps, heading for the streets. Troopers fired their weapons, and anyone who got in their way was run down. The Humvee made it to the other side, climbing up the stairs. It launched into the air, bouncing twice into another building door, where it got stuck. Everything got quiet and the troopers started to ease out with their weapons trained on the Humvee. Then, four metal balls came flying out of the top of the gun turret.

A trooper saw the grenades and yelled for cover. Fortunately, no troopers were caught in the blast, but a single figure scramble over the gun turret laughing and firing his weapon.

"You fools thought you could be sneaky!" he screamed."Ha, ha. You thought you could catch us off guard, but you won't. You won't. You won't get our world. Do you hear me? You won't get our world. Ha, ha!" His laughter echoed as he scrambled over debris into the warehouse.

"Damn. Snipe team. One terrorist made it in. End it," ordered Moore.

Moore was about to order an advance when the second terrorist popped up and grabbed the fifty. Swinging it around, he chambered a round and fired at anything that moved. Moore glanced around the corner only to be driven back by rounds being hammer headed into the corner where his head was just a moment ago.

"Haley, would you please take this guy out so we can get into the damn building?" asked Moore.

"Good as done, Colonel," Haley responded.

Glancing around the corner, she saw the terrorist swing the weapon to his left. Taking a step out, she brought her weapon to her shoulder. Her laser sights homed in on her target. The little red dot stopped at his forehead and fired.

"I sentence you all to..." He never finished the sentence as his head jerked back and he dropped out of view into the Humvee. Like the others, his suicide vest exploded in the Humvee. Moore stepped out from the alley.

"Damn, good shot, Haley. Let's move, people. We have one more and I want him dead before he does more damage," said Moore. As they moved towards the building, more explosions could be heard inside."Get him and kill him."

After throwing his last grenades, the terrorist came running out."You can't stop me. Nobody can stop me. Ha, ha. I will save my beloved planet Earth. Watch me. For I have seen who you really are, monsters, and I promise you will not leave this moon. Ha, ha, ha. And my beloved family will be safe."

Troopers came out of hiding, firing at him. He kept laughing and firing back, knocking down one after another. He knew he was powerful and they couldn't touch him. Finally, he came to the launcher and computer.

"See? You couldn't stop me," he said.

His hands flew over the keyboard and he hit enter. The screen showed launching projectiles."I did it, I did it. I saved my planet and my family." He turned his head to see troopers he killed and more that were coming towards him. A madman's laugh broke out."You are too late. It is done." A bright flash of light appeared in his eyes and his last thought was,"I saved my family," as everything melted away.

***

Moore made it through the rubble and the hallway to exit out into the main warehouse. He stopped to take in the scene. He noticed on the left corner of the building a hole was cut into the floor. Out of that hole in the floor was a big pipe with two tables on either side. A laptop was on one table, but he couldn't make out what the long object was on the other.

"Haley, what does that object look like to you on that table?" he said.

She looked over at the device on the table and studied it for a minute."I'm not an engineer, but that looks like something you put in water mains for inspections. You can see the camera in the front and you can also deliver a bomb with it," she discerned.

"I thought as much. Please contact Evans and ask him to check the serial number on it. I bet you that is the equipment the construction company that did all the pipes for this space station was bitching about," said Moore.

"Roger that, sir," answer Haley.

Moore looked around and saw a medic checking the terrorist. He walked over towards the medic."is he dead?" he said.

The medic looked up."He's dead, sir. Funny thing, Colonel. When I got to him, he was still alive and he mumbled that he had saved his family and Earth."

"Really? Well in his mind he did save his family and Earth, but you have to remember he was a madman. The people he killed and mutilated is proof of that," said Moore."

"You're right, sir," answered the medic.

"Pardon me, Colonel."

Moore turned to see Sun."Captain. Good to see you. Are you through blowing holes in my base?" joked Moore.

"I am, sir." Sun grinned at him.

The smile in his eyes and on his face faded."Let's hear your report," he said with a sad voice.

"As of now, sir, we have twenty-three dead, ten critical, and eighteen wounded. They are being transferred as we speak, sir," reported Sun.

Moore took off his helmet and Sun saw the pain and sorrow in his face."Damn, good troopers gone. All right, Sun, get the engineers down here. I want that launcher disassembled, and have them check where that pipe goes. Also, check that other area where you almost blew a hole in the floor. Have a security detail here around the clock. No one come down here till I say so. No one, Captain."

"Yes, sir," said Sun, calling for her company leaders.

Haley turned."Colonel, Sergeant Major would like a word," she said.

Moore nodded."Go, Sergeant Major."

"Bringing you up to date, I have one Miss Sandhill and Gunny heading to take out Mr. William Scott. He won't be giving any more information to the enemy. He knew they were there and was headed to the transport tubes. They secured his apartment, office, and all other accommodations. The Computer Lab is not happy, but there's nothing they can do. I sent Jessie home to get some sleep. She left all her gear here and I have them secured, sir. She makes a fine officer," said Mary Ann.

"I think so, too. Is that all?" ask Moore.

"Oh, I also sent a report on a secure line to General Chayton. Jessie had the location where they sent all their information to. The General will take care of it and will be waiting for your report."

"Good. Was there anything else?"

She paused."Yes, sir. I found another note on my desk."

"I'm not surprised. What do they say?" He asks.

"'Colonel, we're glad you could stop the terrorist and sorry about your people. You probably noticed that we sent back the three we took. We did not harm them in any way. I give you my word. The young computer expert Jessie is very good and she will find other little surprises on the chip. Use them well and wisely, Colonel. It is a gift from us. A friend,'" Mary Ann conveyed.

"All right, that's interesting. Do they really think I'm going to believe that bull? Make sure medical does a security one medical check on all three of them. Do not let the families know they have been found yet. I want to make damned sure they're fine before they go back to their families. As for our so-called friends, I still want to know how the hell they know about the terrorists, and not to mention how the terrorists got all that equipment on this base. Unfortunately, now they know about Jessie. Mary Ann, place one of your young ladies with her for now."

"I have the perfect one in mind, and I'll send her over in the morning. Colonel, Jessie has informed me she would like to join the military as an officer. Between me and you, we don't want to lose this one, sir. She's brilliant."

"Yes. She surprised me. You do that, Mary Ann. And have her paperwork show that I'm her sponsor."

"Will do Colonel," answer Mary Ann.

"I wonder who the Hell these people are?"

"That's the million-dollar question. sir."

"Million-dollar question my ass, anything else?"

Mary Ann paused."He left a P.S., sir."

"How come I get the feeling I'm not going to like this?" said

Moore.
"'P.S. welcome to the moon, neighbor.'"

HALLORAN'S MINE

By
Aaron Bittner

The bartender refilled the whiskey glass and handed it over.

The little lounge was empty except for the two of them, par for the course for midmorning. The bartender, a young man in his twenties, tried to look busy wiping glasses as he studied the customer. The man across the bar was maybe thirty-five and tall, with dark hair and a self-contained manner. He had an old, puckered scar across his left cheekbone.

Halloran said nothing, but took a cigar out of his jacket pocket and snipped off the end.

"Hey, buddy. If you light that thing up, I'll have to ask you to leave," said the bartender.

"Do you like cigars?" Halloran asked the man.

"Well yeah, but –"

"Ain't nobody here but you and me," Halloran said. "I won't tell if you won't." He took out another cigar and handed it to the bartender. The man hesitated for a moment, then smiled and took it.

"A Padrón. Not bad. You don't see these every day." The bartender sniffed the cigar appreciatively.

"I'm celebrating," Halloran told him.

"What's to celebrate?"

"I just got a new job. Looks like a fresh start for Zane Halloran. Cheers," he said, and lit up.

The bartender reached under the bar, retrieved a heavy glass ashtray, and set it between them.

Halloran exhaled, letting the mouthful of smoke slowly drift as he spoke. "I won't be able to get this kind of stuff again until I come back. If I come back."

"Come back? From where?"

Halloran smiled a quick little smile. "That's classified," he said. "But I'd be lying if I told you the trip didn't scare me some."

"Why's that?"

"Because I know some things." Halloran knocked back the whiskey and set the glass down. "Sometimes it's better not to know."

***

He was traveling light, just one bag with a change of clothes and a few very carefully chosen pieces of equipment. His credentials were in a zipped inner pocket of his jacket, along with one more Padrón. He knew there was no way in hell he could light it up at the moon base - the smoke would play hell with the air processing systems and set off all kinds of alarms - but he brought it along anyway as a promise to himself.

I will carry this cigar with me and smoke it when my feet are on the ground again, he thought. *It would be a shame to waste such a good cigar.*

The one bag made it easy to manage when he stepped out of the taxi at the spaceport main gate. There it was, the North American Space Authority's launch and landing facility, and at that moment thought to be the only one of its kind in the world. The face the spaceport presented to the world was bright, polite, purposeful - a façade of clean lines and unambiguous rectangles with golden mean proportions. It conveyed a shining optimism. It was a physical representation of the idea that not even the sky was a limit anymore.

Since NASA had come under the jurisdiction of the Joint Chiefs, most of the staff work was done by soldiers like the ones that met him at the admission checkpoint, just inside the front doors.

"Good afternoon, sir," said the lieutenant with the data terminal. He was white, young, scrubbed, and had a fresh haircut. "State your business please."

"I'm here to board a transport to the lunar base."

"I'll need two forms of ID, your gate pass, and your boarding authorization."

"They're in my coat pocket," Halloran said has he reached deliberately inside his jacket. The other soldier, the one with the submachine gun, watched carefully, impersonal but intent, like a catcher waiting for a pitch. Halloran slowly retrieved his card case and opened it, revealing his credentials. The clerk scanned them efficiently and noted that all was in order. The name on his tag was Kilby.

"Luggage?" Kilby said.

"Just this," Halloran said, indicating his ruck.

After weighing the bag, the clerk noted, "Sir, you have a cargo allowance of 150kg. This bag is only ten percent of that. Is something missing?"

"The cargo allowance was on Colonel Walker's authorization," Halloran explained. "He suspects I'm going to need lots of equipment they don't have up there already. If I get there and agree, I'll send for it then."

The soldier made a notation in the data terminal. "Very good, sir. Now, if you'll put the bag on the conveyor -"

"Lieutenant Kilby, I have to ask you to check the bag by hand," Halloran said.

"Sir?" said Kilby. The sergeant with the submachine gun blinked.

"There's sensitive equipment in here that reads EM fields. I'd prefer that it not be X-rayed."

Kilby's eyes narrowed.

"It's a legitimate request," Halloran observed, noting the regs posted at the door.

"So it is," said Kilby after a moment. "If you'll open the bag for me, we'll have a look."

Kilby removed items from the bag one by one. A few electronic instruments, a pack of disposable razors, clothes. One of the items was a little felt bag with a drawstring. "Sir, please open that for me," Kilby said.

Halloran opened the pouch and handed it back. Kilby poured the contents out into a plastic tray; the pouch held only a little enameled brass pin. Kilby turned it to see the front, looking puzzled.

The sergeant wasn't puzzled. His eyes were wide as he opened his mouth and "That's a Trondheim unit citation!" tumbled out.

You could practically hear the click as Kilby's eyes snapped to Halloran's face. "Sir...you were at Trondheim?"

"I was a SeaBee. A bulldozer jockey," Halloran said.

"And that scar, sir...?" Kilby asked, his eyes flicking to Halloran's cheek.

"Yes," Halloran said, and nothing more.

Kilby quickly put the pin back in the felt pouch and repacked Halloran's ruck.

"Sir, if there's anything I can do for you, just let me know. Ask for Lieutenant Kilby," he said.

"Or Sergeant Cobb," the soldier with the subgun said.

Fifteen minutes later, Halloran was boarding the shuttle. As he sank into the acceleration couch, he closed his eyes and thought pleasant thoughts.

On the ground, Kilby asked, "How did you know that pin?"

"My mom's got one at the house," Cobb replied. "The DOD sent it to us with my uncle's personal effects."

***

It was a two-day trip, and Halloran was the only passenger; the rest of the shuttle cargo was freight. During the transit, Halloran used his tablet and satellite link to brush up on lunar geology and a few other select topics he thought might be useful, and then some extra things just because he was bored. All pertained in one way or another to the moon.

He was deep into an article on a proposed model for sublunar rock formations when the word came that they were about to land. He felt the thrusters fire as the shuttle made its final deceleration, and a gentle bump as it touched down.

He had been briefed on the disembarkation procedure. As he stood up and walked through the passenger lock, he felt his body adjusting to the low gravity. At home, he weighed 85kg; here he was only 14, and had to move deliberately to keep his feet on the ground. The passenger lock was cramped, a narrow corridor four meters long, and every surface was metal. He felt his ears pop as the pressure in the lock equalized to base normal, and then the environment light turned green and the entrance door slid open.

"Mr. Halloran, welcome to Luna," a voice said as he entered the base. "How was the trip?"

The speaker was a young woman in fatigues. She had a dark buzz-cut and was all business as she noted Halloran's arrival on her tablet.

"It went as expected," he reported. "Which is good. We space travelers hate surprises."

The woman nodded, smiled briefly. "Yes we do," she agreed. "We have retrieved your bag, so if you'll follow me, I'll direct you to your quarters."

Halloran followed her through a freight staging area and deeper into the base. "I have to apologize in advance for the minimal accommodations," she said. "We're a little short on luxuries. I'm Tech Specialist Brantley, and I have been assigned to assist you while you're here."

"Oh really?"

"Anything we can do to help you do your job is well worth it," Brantley said. "You're mission-critical, sir, not to mention expensive."

"Colonel Walker didn't have to pick me," Halloran replied. "I named a rate that I thought would run him off."

"Nobody comes to Luna unless they are the very best at what they do. If Colonel Walker could have found a better mining engineer, he never would have called you."

Halloran wasn't sure what to make of that.

***

At 0900, Halloran followed Brantley to his mission briefing in Colonel Walker's office. As soon as Brantley reported to his orderly that the engineer had arrived, Colonel Walker's door burst open.

"Come in, Halloran," the colonel ordered. "Welcome to Mare

Imbrium, Luna. Have a seat. This won't take long."

Guy Walker was physically large and imposing, square-jawed, perhaps fifty, a former football player only lately gone soft. His office was spacious in an installation where a square foot of floor was worth literally millions of dollars. He gestured to a metal folding chair for Halloran, and parked himself behind a vast desk.

"What have you heard about this mission, Halloran?"

Halloran considered a moment. "Precious little, Colonel. Only the NASA press releases."

"So you don't know why you're here?" Walker prodded.

"I'm a mining engineer, Colonel. Therefore, you have a mining problem that you need solved. We're in an environment that has never been mined before, in a kind of operation that we have never before attempted, so your problem is something you didn't anticipate. You didn't haggle over my rate and you wanted me immediately, so you're on a short schedule," Halloran observed. "Am I getting warm?"

"So far so good. Why didn't I get someone from the Corps of Engineers? They're cheaper and quicker."

"That's easy. Those guys are all by the book. Here there is no book - you need someone who can think on his feet."

"Good enough. So now I'll give you the particulars. Operation Green Cheese was devised to tunnel into the lunar surface, starting with vertical shafts and then branching laterally into galleries at regular intervals. The work was to start with an autonomous drone, configured to burn downward and blow the tailings to the surface through a recovery duct. The tailings are processed into raw material, yielding mainly silicon, iron, and oxygen, along with a handful of other elements. Those other elements, especially the lanthanum and rubidium, are what we're after. We ship that home. We use the iron and silica for surface construction and the oxygen for breathing, and the shaft and later the galleries become new real estate for the colony base. The mining process leaves about a centimeter of glassy slag on the internal surfaces, durable and air-tight. All it takes is energy, which we have plenty of."

"So far so good."

"You'd think. That's how it went, anyway, until 13 May...Tuesday, two weeks ago. That's when the drone started sending back some anomalous instrument readings. We assumed they were calibration issues until we stopped the drone and attempted a pressure test at six hundred meters."

"And found…?" Halloran prompted.

Colonel Walker scowled. "The shaft won't hold air," he replied.

Halloran's eyes widened. "What?"

"We were shooting for a tenth of an atmosphere as a proof-of-concept. We only managed to peak the pressure at zero point oh oh five, and that bled off within an hour."

"But that doesn't make…" he trailed off, his mind racing.

"Sense. I know," said the colonel. "But we still proceeded according to plan until late Wednesday at 21:13. That's when we lost contact with the drone."

"Wireless connection?"

"Cable. We reeled in the busted end."

"Any signs of seismic activity?" Halloran probed.

"The project survey states that Mare Imbrium is stable, and has been for a long time."

That's not what I asked, thought Halloran, but he kept that thought to himself. Instead, he said, "Is there a geology report I can review?"

Walker turned to his tablet, tapping on its glass surface, then looked up. "Mannheim's report is in your inbox," he said. "Anything else?"

"I'd like to talk to your current technology team. Who is your chief mining engineer?"

"You are."

"Before me."

"Skeller," the colonel said with some distaste. "Evan Skeller. He's unavailable for comment."

"Unavailable? Why's that?"

"That's classified information."

"Working on something else now, I guess," Halloran surmised. Walker didn't respond. "I'll want to go see it."

Walker nodded. "Brantley can get you fitted and checked out on a pressure suit."

"I should talk to the geologist first."

Walker nodded. "I'd advise you to move fast, then. Ask Brantley. She'll find him for you."

***

A few minutes later, Brantley led Halloran through one of the longer corridors on the base to the geologist's quarters. A tag next to the door said HORST MANNHEIM. Brantley knocked.

"Enter," came a distracted-sounding voice from within. They opened the door to find a thin man of medium height, with pale skin and grizzled-looking hair, in the middle of packing a rucksack.

"You would think that with only one bag it would be simple to pack," he said over his shoulder as he rolled up a shirt.

Brantley said, "Doctor Horst Mannheim, project geologist. Mannheim, meet Zane Halloran, mining engineer."

"Oh?" said Mannheim, looking up briefly, then returning to his work. "Best of luck to you."

"I'll take all the luck I can get," Halloran replied,. "But I like data too. What can you tell me about the geology of the mine site?"

The geologist paused for a moment, considering. "The mine site is classic Mare Imbrium basalt for base rock, no hydration of course, twenty percent ferric oxide, pretty high titanium content. Of course it's the KREEP that brought us here; concentrations of 30 PPM rubidium, sometimes more - a LOT more - in localized veins."

"KREEP," Halloran mused. "Potassium, rare-earth elements, phosphorus."

"You've done some homework," said Mannheim, resuming his packing.

"Still doing it," Halloran observed. "Are there caverns on the site?"

"I'll assume you aren't referring to leached karst caves. My official report states that there are no cavities of detectable size within the range of the planned excavation."

"Doctor Mannheim, I've read the official report," said Halloran, impatient. "I need to know what's there."

"You'll notice I'm packing," said the geologist, and nobody spoke for a moment.

"Walker's drone design is sound. I've been over it. I believe the fused shaft wall should have been tighter than a bell jar. It should have sealed any microfissures in the rock as it passed through."

"No argument here," said Mannheim.

"The drone was autonomous, yes? So was it programmed to deal with voids in the substrate?"

"Anything under a centimeter wide would have been sealed off as a matter of course."

"That's not what I asked," observed Halloran.

"There were provisions in the drone control code for what to do if it encountered larger voids," said the geologist.

"So what happened?"

"That code was commented out of the operational version of the program."

Halloran scowled. "Why was that, Doctor?"

"Because the official report states that there are no cavities of detectable size within the range of the planned excavation."

"Doctor Mannheim, isn't that kind of crazy?" said Halloran outright.

Mannheim closed the zipper on his rucksack with some difficulty, then shouldered the bag. "You've just got to start asking the right questions. I've got to go now. Shuttle to catch."

"But why would someone want to hide the fact that there were preexisting cavities in the rock here?"

"That's a great one to go on with," said Mannheim. With that, he strode down the corridor and past them, and was gone.

That doesn't make any sense, Halloran thought, but he said nothing to Brantley.

***

Two hours later, Halloran and Brantley were exiting the utility airlock. Halloran was fascinated by his first walk on the moon's natural surface. The stark shapes of raw rock stood out in light gray against the black background of space. The sun was low on the lunar horizon, throwing inky shadows. The gray, ashy lunar soil varied; some felt like the driest, softest dust, and in other areas he could feel it crunch under his feet like gravel.

As they crossed the lunar surface toward the mine shaft, Halloran ignored the smell of sour sweat that infused his suit.

Brantley carried an equipment tote. A small gantry crane stood over the tunnel, a yawning hole four meters square that dropped off into the blackest darkness.

Halloran keyed his suit radio. "Got a light?" he asked.

Brantley produced a high-intensity spotlight from the tote, and Halloran shone it directly down the shaft. The tunnel dropped far off into the distance, its ruler-straight sides a glistening obsidian. There was no sign of the drone. A thrill of excitement passed through him as he stared down into the mystery of that deep black pit.

Halloran stepped back from the tunnel and looked around, then up at the gantry crane.

"You checked out on this equipment?" he asked.

Brantley stammered. "Y-yes, I am."

"What's the range on these suit radios?"

"A couple of miles, line-of-sight. What are you thinking, sir?"

"Drop that headache ball down a couple meters, please."

Brantley stepped to the controls and brought the overhaul ball and its hook down level with the surface.

"Now bring it a meter and a half to the left."

"Sir, did you hear anything I told you during your pressure suit training? If you spill your air out here, you're dead. You don't go down a six-hundred-meter mine shaft standing on a headache ball with no plan, no backup, and no safety gear," Brantley objected. "That's idiotic. You don't get a do-over."

"Understood. I'll be careful. Now get the ball over to the side, please."

"Mr. Halloran, if you get killed on my watch it'll be the end of my career," she said. "I'm supposed to keep you safe."

"This is the moon, Brantley. There's no such thing as safe."

"Maybe not, but there is such a thing as stupid, sir." Even so, her touch on the control panel brought the ball and hook to the edge of the pit.

Halloran rummaged in the tote and came up with a safety strap. He clipped one end to the harness built into the suit, and the other end to the crane cable. "There," he said. "Happy?"

"Happy I'm not your mother," Brantley growled.

"Me too, Brantley," Halloran observed as he stepped lightly onto the overhaul ball. "Lower away."

She followed her orders.

***

As the heavy ball began its descent, Halloran activated an instrument on his belt, and keyed his personal recorder.

"Project Green Cheese mission log. It's 21:10 on Monday, 26 May. I have started my initial descent, safety-rigged to a crane cable. I have activated my inertial tracker, which will log my location in three dimensions during the trip."

He turned on his suit's external light and looked around.

"Ten meters in, the walls of the shaft are as expected. A gray-black slag with a glassy surface. It's so featureless that it's difficult to tell that I'm descending."

In another minute, Brantley's voice broke in. "How is it down there, sir?"

"Dark, Brantley. I'll let you know when something changes."

"You've got an hour and forty-eight minutes of air, and it will take you about four minutes to get to the bottom of the hole, and four minutes back. Heavy exertion will reduce your dwell time."

"Noted. Thank you." Halloran was also keeping an eye on his air supply.

Ninety seconds later, Halloran's barked order came over the radio circuit: "Halt descent!" and Brantley stopped the cable reel.

"Back up about two meters."

Down in the hole, Halloran was looking at something he didn't understand. A spray of irregular cavities, none larger than the tip of his finger, were visible across all four walls of the shaft. He looked closely, but could see nothing more to report. The holes went deeper than his eye could follow. He pressed at the edge of one with a gloved thumb, and a small chip of slag broke off and fell away into the darkness.

"Mission log continued," Halloran said into his recorder. "I'm seeing holes in the walls of the shaft, on the order of five hundred holes ranging in size from two to fifteen millimeters across, irregular in shape. The slag is attenuated near the edge of the holes, suggesting that the mining drone passed through some preexisting porosity in the substrate. This explains where Walker's air went."

Overhead, Brantley was about to burst. "Sir, what is it? Are you all right?"

Halloran keyed the radio. "Fine, Brantley. Resume descent."

As the ball he was standing on began dropping again, Halloran's foot shifted, and, with the rock dust on the sole of his boot, he lost his footing and fell. His right hand had been on the radio controls, and he felt the cable slip out of his left. Before he knew what was happening, he was falling. Not fast, but fast enough that when he came to the end of the safety strap he heard a ping conducted through his suit as the clip that attached him to it gave way.

His heart racing, he began a slow count. If he made it to ten before he hit bottom, his mission was over. He tried very hard to make his body go limp as he fell.

"One...two...three...four...five...si-" And the wind was knocked out of him as he landed nearly flat on his back.

Stunned, he lay in the darkness, not moving for a moment, trying to regain his breath, and flexing each limb in turn to see if he was hurt. He noted that his suit integrity alarm had not gone off. It wasn't a fail-safe, but the suit didn't think he'd spilled his air, and that was something. He breathed a sigh of relief.

He looked at the safety strap still attached to his suit harness. The clip had failed at the cable end, and a small piece of it was missing.

Something moved above his left shoulder. He jumped up and found the headache ball, still making its placid journey downward.

"Brantley...halt descent. I'm at the bottom." The ball stopped dropping, its heavy hook lying on a rock slope. *I wasn't lying*, he thought.

Slope?

"Be careful, sir," came the specialist's voice through the darkness.

"You know it," Halloran replied, and turned to play his suit light on his surroundings. Suddenly he felt very vulnerable. *She was right*, he thought to himself. *There is such a thing as stupid.*

He was standing on a slope of dark-gray basalt. Around him was a large empty space, perhaps fifteen meters across, with one end five meters away and the other end descending beyond sight. He looked up, and immediately knew what had happened to the mining drone. It had fallen through the ceiling.

"Mission log continued," he recorded. "Bottom of the shaft opens into a cavity of uncertain dimensions. How this cavity came to be here I have no idea. I knew there was something Mannheim wasn't telling me."

A few meters downslope, the grade leveled out, and that was where the drone had skidded to a halt. He looked it over. It was a small fusion generator in a square cage frame made of high-temp alloy, with plasma cutters arrayed over the lower surface; some of these were smashed and would need to be replaced.

"Brantley," he said, "I found the drone. Minor damage, looks like the inertial safety shut it down. It got snagged on a rock down here, the tether wouldn't pull it back." Under the low gravity, he was able to shift the drone so it could be drawn back up the hole.

"Play out some more cable, I'll tie it on for retrieval." The drone had a hoist point on the frame for just this. Brantley dropped him five more meters of line, and he attached it to the drone.

That done, he turned his back to the drone and shone his suit light further down the slope into the deep darkness beyond. The cavity opened into a truly large space. After a moment, a detail on the wall of the cavern caught his eye...five vertical marks incised on the stone surface.

He stood for a moment, making sure that he was seeing what he thought he was seeing, then he keyed his recorder.

"Mission log continued," he said. "You're not going to believe this."

***

Back on the surface early the next morning, Colonel Walker was not happy. He sat behind his vast desk glaring at Halloran.

"I've read your report," the colonel growled. "There are some things you're going to have to correct."

"What's the issue, Colonel?" Halloran said placidly.

"You found that our mining drone had penetrated a cavern, and then concluded that the cavern was in fact manmade."

"My report does not include the term *manmade*, Colonel."

"Don't screw with me, Halloran. You know what I mean."

Halloran looked the colonel in the eye and said, "Yes I do...but

I'm not certain that *you* know what *I* mean." He paused, and in that brief moment the whirring of the air vent seemed very loud to him. "What I stated was that the cavity at the bottom of your shaft was artificial in origin."

"Aliens?" Walker bit back a laugh. "This is Mare Imbrium, Halloran, not some two-bit space opera. The rock here is igneous, like everywhere else on the moon. We bored through the characteristic olivine basalt into a characteristic magma tube."

"I've seen magma tubes, Colonel. The morphology of this space was not consistent with a magma tube."

"You've seen magma tubes on Earth. This isn't the Earth, in case you hadn't noticed."

I could learn to dislike this guy, Halloran thought.

"I will admit that I'm a mining engineer. Archaeology isn't my area of expertise."

"Lunar archeology isn't *anyone's* area of expertise." The colonel was practically spitting out his words. "And it isn't about to be."

"I saw tool marks, Colonel."

"You saw natural features, Halloran. And that's the end of it."

Halloran said nothing for a moment. The colonel was breathing hard, his face red.

"Am I clear?" said the colonel finally.

"Crystal, sir," said Halloran evenly.

"This mission will continue as planned. We built in a margin for up to three weeks of delay, and that's nearly all gone. From now on this mission will tick along like a Swiss watch. We will hit every mark and meet every goal. Seeing that it does so is why we brought you up here, if you'll remember."

Yes, Halloran decided. *I definitely dislike this guy.*

***

Back in his quarters, Halloran deactivated his pocket recorder and activated his tablet. He made satellite contact and opened a channel encrypted with his own private key. The ping went several minutes before it was picked up on the other end. Halloran was relieved; he wasn't sure it would be.

"Doctor Barnhart," a voice said over the line. It was a

completely professional alto voice that took Halloran back years. He waited for the video to buffer, and in a moment Liz Barnhart's face swam into view.

She looks the same, he thought. Her hair was auburn and tied back, as it always was when she was working. She had full lips, expressive gray eyes, and a strong nose with a spray of freckles. Halloran remembered her legs; her legs went all the way to Columbia University, where she had done post-doctoral work on Mayan inscriptions while he got an engineering degree and tried to make sense of his life after the war.

Her expression was all business even as she recognized him through the data link.

"Zane," she said, and he couldn't read her mood from the word. She frowned at her own tablet. "This link is terrible," she said. "Where are you calling from?"

"In a minute," he answered.

"I'm working, Zane. I don't have time for games."

"I don't know how much vacation time you have saved up," said Zane carefully, "but I bet you're about to take all of it at once."

"Oh really?"

"I'm not kidding, Liz. This isn't a personal call, it's business."

She cocked her head, frowning. Halloran saw two familiar lines appear between her eyebrows.

"I'm committed until August at least," she said. "What's this about?"

"I need an archaeologist. You were the first one that came to mind."

"I'll bet."

"Seriously, Liz. You're qualified, and I need someone I can trust. I wouldn't be calling you otherwise... Believe me."

"Oh, I believe you," she said. "You were always terrific at not calling."

"Liz, you asked where I was calling from. I'm on the moon."

"On the moon? You mean the *moon* moon?" She thought for a moment. "You're at the lunar base?"

"Yes. And I need an archaeologist."

"You need...an..." Her eyes suddenly went wide, and her mouth dropped open as she realized what he was saying. Then it snapped shut again.

"I told you I didn't have time for games," she said.

"This is absolute truth, Liz. I'm going to send you some data files, they include my inertial map of my trip into the mine, and photos of what I saw while I was there. If you decide it's crap, stay home."

"And if not...?"

"...and if not, you get to pioneer a new field: xenoarchaeology."

He checked the clock on his tablet. It only took her seventy-one seconds to decide.

***

While the link was up, Halloran made another call.

"Lieutenant Kilby," he said, "Zane Halloran. Remember me? I need your help with something..."

Halloran spent the next several minutes outlining what he had in mind.

"Not a problem, sir," Kilby said when Halloran had finished. "I'll take care of it."

Halloran thanked him and signed off.

***

For the next two days he helped to oversee continued work at the mineshaft as technical advisor. Based on his advice, they sealed off the cavity with fused basalt and resumed tunneling downward. Halloran was careful to ensure that the rock wall for the repair was thin enough to reopen easily when the time came.

He set up the mouth of the cavity as a staging area, stocking it with extra oxygen, plasma cutters, and various other tools and supplies. Ostensibly this was for Stage II Operations when the galleries were opened, but Halloran had other ideas. He had initially argued that the entire cavity be surveyed and mapped, but Walker was adamant that neither time nor effort could be spared for such work. As far as Walker was concerned, the cave was a complication, and the sooner it could be overcome and forgotten the better.

***

All went well until the next supply shuttle arrived. Halloran met the transport at the personnel lock, with Brantley at his elbow. Several passengers disembarked, all military personnel cycling in to replace their counterparts traveling back to Earth; military personnel worked the Lunar base on a six-month rotation. After the soldiers had come through, the last person off the shuttle was Liz Barnhart.

She saw Halloran and smiled. "Hello, Zane," she said.

Brantley turned to Halloran and did not smile. "What the hell is going on?"

"Tech Specialist Zoë Brantley, I'd like to introduce my colleague Dr. Elizabeth Barnhart. Liz, this is Brantley."

"She wasn't on the passenger manifest," Brantley said, irritated. "Who authorized this?"

"Colonel Walker did," Halloran stated calmly. "And she wouldn't be on the passenger manifest. Check your bill of lading."

Brantley shuffled through documents on her tablet. "Oh, this is rich," she said, scowling. "Doctor Barnhart, you'll be pleased to know that you're referenced in the shuttle's bill of lading as 'Halloran's baggage.'"

The archaeologist barked out a laugh. "You have no idea," she said.

Thank you, Kilby, Halloran thought.

"I'll have to notify the colonel immediately," Brantley declared.

Halloran nodded. It was no more than he expected. Once Liz arrived it was going to hit the fan. Might as well get it over with.

***

It began about the way Halloran thought it would. Halloran, Brantley, and Dr. Barnhart were literally called onto the carpet in the colonel's office.

"Perhaps I have not been communicating clearly, Mister Halloran," the colonel began in a flinty voice. Every syllable dropped from his mouth like a piece of jagged glass. "I understood myself to have given orders that no archaeologist was to be attached to this project."

"Not explicitly, Colonel," Halloran said.

Walker stood for a moment with his jaw clenched, then said, "There. Right there is the communication problem I'm talking about. Brantley here was clear on it; she knew very well what I meant when I briefed her. How unauthorized personnel made it here on our shuttle despite these orders is a mystery to me," and he turned a baleful glare on the unhappy Tech Specialist. "Brantley, do you have anything to say for yourself?"

Brantley was standing at stiff attention, her eyes focused straight ahead. Beads of sweat had appeared on her forehead. She swallowed hard and replied, "No excuse, s-sir. I should have checked cargo documentation as well as the passenger manifest, s-sir."

"Cargo documentation." The colonel squinted. "What the hell does cargo documentation have to do with it?"

"Mining consultant Halloran had the unauthorized personnel delivered here under your authorization for cargo allowance, sir."

Walker's eyebrows shot upward. "Oh, he did? Meaning that he fully knew and understood that shipping up an archaeologist as a passenger would not have been permitted?"

"Presumably, sir."

"No need to presume, Specialist. We have Halloran here to give us the facts of the matter." He turned his baleful gaze on the engineer. "Well?"

Halloran looked him steadily in the eye. "Better to get forgiveness than permission, Colonel."

Walker stalked up to Halloran until his chin was no more than six inches from Halloran's nose. Starting out in a soft gritty monotone, the colonel said, "That's real special. REAL special. And it shows that you know absolutely nothing about me, you useless son of a mother, because if there's one thing anyone in my command will tell you it's that while occasionally you can get permission from me, I will NEVER, EVER, EVER FORGIVE INSUBORDINATION!" Flecks of spittle spattered Halloran's face.

Halloran stood impassively. *I don't report to you,* he thought, but said nothing.

"Don't think I'm going to pay you for this job, Halloran," Walker growled.

"It's a standard GS contract, Colonel. Any dispute about services rendered will be taken up in arbitration."

The colonel stared at Halloran for a moment and something ugly played across his face.

"Well," he said finally, "you may not be under my direct command, Halloran, but I DO command every aspect of base operations. Therefore you will resume your work on the mining project as instructed..." He glanced at Liz. "...and this person will be confined to secure quarters until the very next shuttle arrives, at which time she will be shipped earthside. Understood, Brantley?"

"Yes sir!" Brantley said.

"I want to know the minute she's gone. See to it."

Brantley turned to face Liz. "Yes, sir. Doctor Barnhart, please come with..."

"Colonel Walker." Liz's voice was calm, clear, and oddly striking when she finally broke her silence. "You should be aware of some things before your orders are carried out."

Walker's head rotated to face the archaeologist like a tank turret coming on target. "What?"

"Photographs of the cavern's interior are on file on my university network and at least two other secure servers. They are the basis of an article currently in progress for publication, and I have shared them with several colleagues. I have advised the United Nations of the reason for this trip, and I am here as an authorized representative of UNESCO. Therefore..." Liz took a breath. "...therefore there is nothing to be gained by preventing my access to the site. Your secret is already out."

"That's where you're wrong," said Walker. "We have no secrets here. This is a mining operation that encountered a natural cavity in the rock, and that's all there is to it."

"Then surely there is no harm in my seeing it firsthand," Liz observed.

"Potentially there is quite a bit of harm, Doctor," the colonel replied. "This is Mare Imbrium, Luna, not a Greek ruin. This place has twenty ways to kill you before breakfast, and you have not received any of the requisite training, or qualified through our selection process. While personally I do not give a rat's ass if you want to go down a hole in the moon and die, professionally I don't have the time for the paperwork. So you're staying in quarters until the next shuttle."

Liz, wearing her best poker face, said, "Very well. That being the case, based on the evidence I have seen thus far, I will recommend that this site be designated a UNESCO World Heritage Site pending further investigation. By international law, all industrial and military operations must cease unless and until this recommendation is denied by UNESCO."

Walker laughed. "Nice try, Doc," he said. "We know that's not going to happen. It would take years to resolve."

"Possibly decades," Liz said, and didn't smile.

Walker stared at her for several heartbeats. Halloran discovered he was holding his breath, waiting for the colonel's reaction.

When it came it was almost disappointing. The colonel let out a sigh, seeming to deflate as he did so, and shrugged. "You win, Doctor Barnhart. Should you decide to enter the Project Green Cheese mineshaft, I will not act to prevent it. Understand, however, that doing so is against my most strenuous advice to the contrary."

"Thank you, Colonel," Liz replied.

Walker nodded to Brantley. "Brantley, see that Doctor Barnhart is checked out on a pressure suit. Should she and Halloran decide to visit the mine site, please accompany them on the surface, but do not under any circumstances enter the mine."

"Understood, Sir," the tech specialist said, frowning.

"Dismissed." The colonel turned and sat at his desk as though they were already gone, while the others filed out.

***

Two hours later, the three of them were again walking on lunar soil.

"What do you think of the gravity?" Halloran asked Liz, taking in the surreal black-and-gray landscape around them.

"I'd like it better if it wasn't for the suit."

Halloran noted that even the bulky pressure suit could not manage to conceal her figure. He thought about mentioning it, but instead asked, "What's wrong with the suit?"

"It smells like armpit."

Brantley spoke. If anything, she sounded irritated. "Limited water for laundry, Doctor. And suits are hard to sanitize even back home."

"Yeah, well, I guess a used suit on the moon is like a warm toilet seat. You're glad to have it, but you wonder who was there before you."

Halloran glanced at the front of the suit. "I guess it was Jones," he said, and pointed to a faded ID imprint.

"Hmm. Wonder what happened to Jones?" Liz mused.

"It doesn't add up," Brantley mumbled.

"What doesn't add up, Brantley?"

"Uh...nothing. Never mind," Brantley replied.

"You think they're monitoring the helmet links?" Liz asked.

"Of course they are," Brantley said. "It's SOP. The video feeds from the cameras, too."

"It doesn't matter," said Halloran. "He already doesn't trust us. Let him listen, and watch. Brantley, what's got you worried?"

"The colonel—well, I would be concerned if I were you."

"You think we should abort this trip and go back inside?"

"I think you were idiots to come out here in the first place," Brantley said in a flat, matter-of-fact way. "I'm assigned to you, so I'm under orders to be committed to your safety. Coming out here with the colonel's agreement is dangerous enough. Doing so against his express orders, well—I would have a hard time thinking of something less safe."

"There's no such thing as safe, Brantley," Liz interjected.

Halloran and Brantley exchanged a look, and each knew what the other was thinking. Suddenly Halloran had a thought. "What happened to Jones?" he asked.

Brantley's eyes clouded through the visor. "That's...classified, sir." But she pointed to Liz's midriff. On the left side there was a heavy-duty patch, stitched in place and sealed with polymer cement.

"Suit failure."

"I am not authorized to comment."

"Liz, I'll leave it to you. Do you want to go back, or go on?" Halloran asked.

"Are you nuts? This is the chance of a lifetime. If I went back now I might as well turn in my archaeology card... I'd never be able to look myself in the face again."

"What if it kills you?"

"The other choice is to spend the rest of my life wondering what was down there, and knowing I came this close to it, and didn't find out." Liz set her jaw in the determined way that Halloran remembered, and the engineer knew that nothing in heaven, earth, or even the moon would change her mind.

"If she's committed, so am I," Halloran told Brantley.

"It's decided, then," said Brantley.

They resumed their march to the mine.

***

After Halloran's fall, he had the fabrication shop build an elevator gondola for use with the gantry crane. That made it easier and considerably safer for Halloran and the archaeologist to descend into the mine this time. As they neared the indicated depth, Halloran called over the radio link, "Brantley, halt descent on my mark.... three... two... one... mark."

The gondola came to a halt right at the cavity mouth. The weak illumination of the suit lights only served to make it look that much more dark and forbidding.

"You've each got about an hour and forty minutes of air," came Brantley's voice over the radio.

"Understood, Brantley," Halloran replied. "We will return to this location in not more than sixty minutes for retrieval. Until then we expect to lose radio contact. Halloran out."

"Acknowledged."

"Lose radio contact?" Liz asked.

"Near the entrance, the mineshaft acts like a waveguide and Brantley can hear us. As we move away from the cavity entrance, that effect goes away, and the rock blocks the signal. We won't be able to hear her either."

Halloran stepped off the gondola and looked over the supplies that were staged in the tunnel entrance. Selecting a plasma cutter, he checked the capacitor charge—it was topped off—and activated the unit.

"Stand back." Wielding the cutter like an old-fashioned chain saw, Halloran sliced away the fused rock wall that blocked the entrance as though it were so much cheese. He cut around the perimeter, then nudged the wall in the center with his shoulder. The section of rock tipped briefly, then fell over in slow motion. The great black cavity opened before them.

"Let's go," Liz said, and she strode through the gap, portable floodlight in hand. By the time he had deactivated the plasma cutter and clipped it to his belt, Halloran had to hurry to keep up.

She didn't get far before she stopped short. "Hold up—this is for history, let's get it right." She started going over small pieces of equipment attached to the outside of her suit. "Data recorder...check. Body cam...check. Audio recorder...check. Okay, now lights..." and she activated the portable flood.

***

Ahead of them, the gallery stretched away into the darkness. Though the ceiling was only a few meters above where they stood, they could see that it arched up and away to cover a space the size of an airplane hangar. They couldn't see the far end of it.

"Wow," said Liz.

"That was my thought."

"So what makes you think it's artificial?"

"A few things. One, the room is symmetrical side-to-side. Two, check this out..." He reached for the light, and she handed it to him. He shone it upward. "You see that curve where the wall blends into the ceiling? And it continues to curve overhead? That curve is a catenary, both laterally and lengthwise."

"That doesn't make it artificial," Liz observed. "You see catenary arches in karst caves. What if everything fell away that wasn't in shear?"

Halloran shone the light down on the floor again. "Then where's the stuff that fell?"

"Good point," said Liz. Ahead of them the floor ran smooth and level, with no debris on it except a very thin layer of dust. No rubble indicated a cave-in.

"The catenary curve is good for load bearing; evidence that that arched ceiling didn't happen by accident. Also, I saw these." Halloran directed the light against the side wall to their left. The dust on the floor showed his own footprints from days before, and they walked over them as they approached the wall. Where Halloran was shining the light, there were five ruler-straight vertical lines cut into the rock.

"Look at this," Halloran said, then he spoke for the record. "Five vertical cuts, parallel, all equal in length at approximately ten centimeters, width point five centimeters, separation about one centimeter, probably four millimeters deep. They appear to have been incised with some hard instrument." To Liz he said, "You saw these in my photos."

Liz nodded her head. "I see why you thought this might be artificial."

"*Might* be? How could it be anything else?"

"We're gathering data. It's way too soon to start drawing conclusions."

Halloran rolled his eyes. "Academics..."

Liz didn't look at him. "Engineers," she shot back.

"Let's move on."

They did. As they proceeded, the ceiling arched high above them. Halloran was having a hard time estimating, but the laser rangefinder told him it was one hundred twelve meters above his head.

Ninety meters into the gallery, something caught Halloran's eye. He had given the portable floodlight back to Liz, and she saw the thing ahead of them almost as soon as Halloran did.

"Some sort of pedestal," Liz observed. It was a basalt slab about sixty centimeters high, flat and octagonal. As they approached, they could see a smear in the dust on the floor just this side of the slab. On the top of the slab was a circle of eight holes, each about three centimeters across.

"Look. There's no dust on it."

It was true. Although the thin layer of dust covered the floor evenly all around, there was none on the slab in front of them.

"How old do you think this dust is?" asked Halloran.

"I—I couldn't even begin to formulate an answer," Liz replied. "There's no wind or rain erosion here, no freeze-thaw cycles - in fact, I don't even know why there is dust here at all. I don't know what natural process would create it."

"Unless an artificial process created it..."

"...like construction. Or excavation."

"Right."

"Hey, look at this," Liz said, and stepped around the slab, pointing the light at the floor on the far side. There were more smears in the dust there, and three parallel tracks in the dust that led away into the darkness.

"These look like drag marks," Liz said.

"Three linear marks in the dust on the floor, which appear to have been left when an object was pulled or dragged over the surface," Halloran intoned for the record. "Each is about twenty centimeters wide, and they're a little under a meter apart."

Liz made sure her helmet camera got a good look. "This is incredible. What made these?"

"With any luck, we'll get to find out. Uh..." Halloran paused.

"What?"

"By the clock, we've gone twenty-two minutes since our last time check. To make our sixty-minute rendezvous we've got eight minutes until we turn back."

Liz didn't even look at him. "That means we've got seventy-eight minutes of air," she said through the radio. She was already walking away. Halloran shrugged and followed her.

They walked parallel to the marks in the dust. The streaks continued on, looking for all the world like the tracks of a three-wheeled cart. After perhaps another hundred and ten meters, Halloran noted that the walls were tapering inward with the ceiling arching downward to meet them. Walls and ceiling met at the gallery exit, a passageway perhaps five meters high and just as wide. Liz paused to give her camera a good look, then marched in and onward.

Halloran checked his inertial map. They were two hundred and five meters in and still moving inward, and now the passageway was sloping downward. They progressed along an eight percent grade for several minutes, and another check on his inertial map showed that the passage was curving slightly leftward as they went. Still the layer of dust on the floor was consistent, and still the three streaks continued. Halloran noticed when they passed the thirty-minute mark, but said nothing.

As they walked, from time to time Liz would play the light laterally along the passage walls, looking for whatever might be there to see. There was little of note; the walls were smooth rock.

"I can't help but wonder what this was all for," she said.

"Oh, I'm pretty sure I know."

"You *know*—not unless you got word from whoever built it."

"Eh. Why are *we* here?"

"Minerals. And that's one working theory."

"The only one that makes any sense."

"...and so he commits the classic blunder of interpreting another culture through the lens of his own," Liz intoned.

"And there YOU go assuming that this tunnel is an artifact from another culture."

Liz nodded, reluctantly. "Touché. Still, if we'd been here before, don't you think somebody would know?"

"You'd think. Russians, maybe?"

"You'd know that better than I would. They aren't supposed to have the funds to support an effort like this."

"What we're seeing would be hard to accomplish with our current technology. It would take years."

"Well, shit," Liz said. "Just shit."

Halloran looked up to see that they had entered another gallery. The walls and ceiling were curved as the previous ones had been, but the path forward was blocked by a great pile of rubble. Liz played the light upward toward the ceiling, but the top of the rock fall could not be seen. The slope was very steep, and sloped away and out of sight near the ceiling. What they could see of it was at least eighty meters high, and some of the boulders in the pile were the size of a city bus.

Liz kicked a stone nearby. "You don't know how much I wanted to see where those tracks went," she muttered. The drag marks, if that's what they were, led right up to (and apparently under) the great mound of stone that blocked their way.

Halloran again asked for the floodlight, and played it upward. "I think we can manage it," he said.

"Climb *that*?" Liz was aghast. "Are you out of your mind?" The rock pile was nearly vertical and rose up off the floor like the world's biggest grave marker.

"Quite possibly," Halloran replied, and handed Liz the light. He crouched down as deeply as he could and abruptly leaped upward.

Liz just stared as he came lightly to rest on a basalt ledge some two meters above the floor.

"One-sixth gravity, remember?" he said.

"Right," Liz breathed. "Are you sure this is safe?"

"It's not really safe, no. When you jump up, you'll come down again with the same force you launched yourself with, just like on Earth. The only difference here is you go higher in between, and you have a longer hang time."

Liz bounded upward, and a moment later was standing next to him on the ledge.

"If this pile is from a cave in, why is it so vertical?"

"Angle of repose. It's a lot steeper under low gravity," Halloran said as he took the next jump.

Several leaps and scrambles later, they were almost to the top of the pile when Halloran paused to check his chronometer.

"Uh, Liz, we have to go back."

"Like hell!"

"No, really—we have to go back, and I mean now. By Brantley's calculations we have less than thirty minutes of air left, and that's just enough for us to get back to the base."

"But we have the emergency reserves!" Liz barked testily.

"Which are for emergencies. Which this isn't."

"But look...we're so close!" Liz groaned, playing the floodlight upward. The top of the pile was almost within reach—another couple of jumps and they would be on the other side. The now-irregular ceiling rose up and away into the darkness above them.

"And no doubt that will be a great consolation to you when we *almost* make it back to the base alive," Halloran wryly observed. "At least we've got my pictures and your paper, and the UN notification to console us. They'll name the UNESCO site in our honor."

"Oh, about that—I was bluffing."

"You were *bluffing*? So..."

"So nobody knows what's down here but you and me."

Suddenly a strange voice broke in on their radio circuit: "...and

163

that's the way it will stay. Engage targets!"

Instantly the space around them was full of zipping rock chips that clattered against their helmets. Halloran saw flashes from the floor below. Instantly it was fifteen years ago, and he was in battle.

He seized Liz by the waist and threw her upward with all his strength. "Take cover!" he shouted, and dove behind the nearest boulder between him and the floor. As he did so he felt something tug at his left arm, and his suit integrity alarm began warbling in his ear like a demented songbird as his air bled out into the space of the gallery. He grabbed madly for his supply pouch, ripped open an emergency patch, and slapped it on his sleeve. It wouldn't hold forever, he knew, but it was much better than nothing. In a moment, the suit alarm shut off, and Halloran turned off his suit light.

"Liz...lights out!" he said, and without answering Liz shut off the portable flood and her suit light. Halloran was looking around madly in that moment, and in the split second before the light went out he saw what he wanted: the next ledge. Without stopping to think—if he thought about it he would never do it, he knew - he leaped for the ledge and made it, tumbling quickly down to take cover again. He saw a spotlight from down below playing over the rock pile right at the spot he had just been, and saw chips of rock spray from the spot as bullets cascaded into it.

How much air do I have now? he wondered to himself, but there was nothing that could be done about it, so he put it out of his mind. He was in battle, he was unarmed, he was probably outnumbered, and the odds were stacked against them.

What are my assets?

An answer came to him: *Height.* He was higher than they were.

As the light played over the rock face from down below, Halloran used its dim glow to inspect the closest boulders. Two rocks down from the ledge he was on, there was a chunk of basalt the size of a beach ball. On earth he could never have budged it, but here it could be managed. He put himself behind it with his back against the rocky pile, braced his feet against it, and with all the strength he could muster he shoved it with his legs, launching it outward and downward toward the light.

As it fell through the spotlight's beam he heard "Incoming!" over the suit radio, and the light played wildly as its owner scrambled for cover. Liz must have been watching and figured out what was going on, for without saying anything to him she started launching stones from the top of the pile. While this was going on, Halloran felt around until he found a stone about the size of a baseball. When the next big rock started down—and it was *big*; Liz had gotten lucky and found one on the edge of tipping that was almost the size of a small car—Halloran popped up out of cover and launched his stone at the spotlight. He wasn't sure if it was a good throw and didn't remain standing to see, but he had played a lot of ball as a kid, and the throw felt good as it left his hand.

He was gratified a moment later to hear a loud CRACK in his suit radio, followed by the idiot warble of a suit alarm that quickly faded out as the air left the owner's helmet.

Bull's eye. Hit him in the face shield. One down.

"Sergeant, Lockwood's down!"

"Leave him," came the other, now-familiar voice. "You two retreat out of range and engage your weapons from a distance."

Someone down below had retrieved the spotlight, for it once again began playing over the rock face. No more bullets were flying in, but Halloran stayed well under cover.

Now the enemy had retreated out of stone's throw range.

So there are three of them left, Halloran thought to himself. *What are my assets?*

He looked around him and noticed the plasma cutter hanging at his belt.

It was adjustable.

He turned the unit over and pulled a cover off the underside of the machine. The factory settings were limited, but you could override them if you knew how to set the right microswitches, and Halloran did. The stock reach had a three-meter maximum. Halloran overrode that; he set the maximum reach to two hundred meters, the duration to five hundredths of a second, and the power output to six hundred percent of the stock maximum. This kind of abuse would burn out the beam generator within a hundred power cycles or so, but that was academic. The power capacitor could only fire the unit that way for, at most, twenty shots.

Now instead of a rock saw, he had an energy weapon. It was crude, unreliable, and had no sights, but it was something.

Halloran thought about the bullets that had been knocking

stone chips off the rock pile. They were using good old-fashioned guns with good old-fashioned bullets, and though they were adapted for use in space, they still used a chemical propellant to fire. *Hmm.*

He reached down to his utility belt and retrieved his hand light. Easing himself up and over the edge of the nearest boulder, he got the plasma cutter into position, activated the hand light, and tossed it bouncing down the side of the slope.

Instantly he saw flashes burst out below him. He picked the target to his left and took his best shot; the blue plasma cutter beam missed badly high and to the right. He adjusted and fired again; this one was closer. He "walked" the next two shots into his target and abruptly the flashes from that spot ceased.

"Troopers report," came the command voice.

"Conyers," came a voice back, then silence.

"Trent? Trent, report!"

Halloran could taste the air turning stale in his helmet. *This is it, then,* he thought, but kept going.

He spoke into the mic. "Trent's down, Sergeant," he said. "That's two men you've lost this mission. I advise you to retreat."

The reply was as colorful as it was obscene.

"Really, Sergeant. We don't have enough air to make it back topside. Just leave and we'll buy the farm soon enough. Stick around and you're likely to lose another man, or even yourself."

There was silence on the other end. Halloran could tell his air was getting worse, and resisted the urge to pant, which would only make him run out of oxygen that much sooner. Just as he began to see spots he flipped open a switch cover on his left wrist and activated his emergency reserves. It wouldn't get him back to base, but it would buy him a few more minutes.

"Halloran," came the sergeant's voice. "You just cost us two good men. When you breathe your last breath down in this hellhole you think about that, you son of a bitch."

Halloran said nothing, but waited.

"We'll be back in a day to pick up the bodies...theirs and yours. Conyers, retreat." Halloran watched as the spotlight made its way back through the entrance and faded out of sight.

Halloran sat for a moment and took stock. A moment later Liz was next to him, suit light back on.

"You okay?" she asked. The two worry lines had reappeared between her eyebrows.

"Bullet clipped my suit," he replied. "I spilled most of my air, now I'm on emergency reserve."

"That's good for what, ten minutes?"

"Yeah."

"Okay. On your feet, trooper."

Halloran looked up at her like she was crazy. She stood up and took him by the hand.

"I said on your feet," she repeated, and pulled him to a standing position.

Well, hell, he thought. *If she's got hope I might as well play along.*

"The first thing we have to do is get ourselves down off this rock pile. We go down the same way we came up."

"Going down will be harder."

"Ain't like it's optional." She carefully stepped over the edge to land on the next rock down.

Between them they leapfrogged down the rubble heap. They were almost to the bottom when an audible rumble conducted itself up through their boots, and then they felt the entire pile begin to shift and move.

"Jump free!" Halloran took Liz by the hand and leapt into space. "Keep moving when you hit the ground!" he said as they flew. Together they fled away from the shifting, boiling pile of rocks as it came crashing down behind them.

Finally, when it was over, Halloran turned to Liz beside him on the cavern floor. "You okay?"

"Yeah—what *was* that?"

"Don't know, but I bet our friends set off a demolition charge in the upper cavern."

"Well, we'll deal with that when we get to it," Liz said.

Yeah, Halloran thought. *Whatever makes you happy.*

They got to their feet and headed back toward the gallery entrance. As they were heading out, Halloran noticed something on the floor off to his left. His suit light soon showed him that it was Trent, or what remained of him. The thigh of his suit had been flayed open by the plasma cutter, and flakes of his freeze-dried blood lay around him on the gallery floor.

"Sorry, Trent. You were only doing your job." He bent down and turned the soldier's body over.

Bingo, he thought to himself, and went to work.

"What are you doing?"

"I'm detaching Trent's auxiliary rebreather. He clearly doesn't need it anymore, but I could really use it."

The auxiliary rebreather was a supplemental oxygen unit carried on the belt in back like an outsized fanny pack. The military suits used them to provide a backup oxygen system or additional capacity for extended missions.

"Help me with this," Halloran said, holding the rebreather out to Liz. "I'm getting woozy..." And then the world went very dark very quickly.

***

"Zane! Zane? Are you okay?"

Someone was shaking him.

"Zane! Wake up!"

He blinked and opened his eyes, struggled to focus. "Liz," he croaked.

She was kneeling by him. "Thank God! I wasn't sure I'd got it right."

"The rebreather..."

It lay on the rock next to him, its spring-loaded air hose tied in to his own oxygen system with a pair of quick-release couplings.

"Yeah, that's it. Good job, Liz."

"Yeah, yeah. Now on your feet. We still have to get out of here."

Halloran climbed to his feet and looked around. "I wonder what Brantley's thinking right now," he mused.

"She's thinking we're dead. She will have heard the sergeant's report."

"Yeah. Probably so. Well, then," Halloran said, blinking the fatigue out of his eyes, "Won't she be surprised!"

***

They were both surprised when they turned the last corner into the upper gallery. Halloran had thought they had used explosives to seal off the tunnel; instead, they had used a shaped charge of high explosive to destroy the stone octagon. A few large chunks of it lay near its original location but the rest was shattered, a shallow crater left where it had been.

"What the...?"

"Those bastards!" Liz growled. "How many of those plinths do you suppose we'll see again in our lifetimes?"

"Must have been on the colonel's orders, but God only knows what *he* was thinking."

"He was thinking that something was complicating his mission," said Liz. "I know the type. I've seen them before. I know you have too."

Halloran stared off into the darkness. *Yes I have,* he thought. *Indeed I have.*

***

They approached the main vertical shaft on foot, lost in their own thoughts, when Liz started hyperventilating.

"Zane!" she panted. "Help me! I'm... I'm out of air!"

Zane reached for her left arm and grabbed for the emergency reserve switch. It was already activated. "You've used up your reserves!"

"No point...no point in...worrying you...about it..." she huffed.

Halloran checked the readings on his rebreather unit, then detached his quick connects and linked them up rapidly to Liz's suit. As her breathing returned to normal, Liz cried, "But your suit! What are you doing for air?"

"The suit holds two minutes' worth of air for the average man, and I can hold my breath for another two. Breathe," he said, and she did.

"We can share it."

"Yeah, but not for long. Every time you disconnect and reconnect it in a vacuum, you're losing some air. Now, you good for a minute?"

Liz nodded, and Halloran switched the rebreather back to his own suit to replenish his own supply. This wasn't a tenable situation, he knew, but what were his options?

No, he thought. *The first question is: 'What are my assets'?*

He thought for a moment, then he remembered the stores he had stocked at the tunnel entrance.

Bottled oxygen. "Let's get moving again. We have to get to the elevator."

***

At the tunnel entrance, Halloran took stock of the equipment that was left. The soldiers hadn't touched it, being intent on their mission, and there were three big cylinders of oxygen like welder's bottles arrayed in the doorway. It was the work of a moment to connect to them using the standard couplings for field replenishment, and both of their suits were supplied to capacity. Halloran was pleased to see that his suit patch was holding up fine for the moment.

"Okay, now what?" Liz asked, and Halloran's heart sank.

She was looking up the vertical shaft. There was no gondola and no cable dangling down. They were six hundred meters down a hole in the moon with nobody coming to get them, and the only thing the bottled O_2 had bought them was time.

"The sergeant will be back in a day," said Liz. "We'll deal with him and ride the gondola back to the surface."

"We got terribly lucky a little while ago. We can't depend on getting that lucky again."

"So what can we do? We can't just stay here," Liz said, and he had to agree. "Can we climb our way out?"

He looked at the shaft walls doubtfully. "The sides are like glass."

"Cut steps with the plasma cutter?"

"Good idea," Halloran said, "but I'm pretty sure we'll run out of capacitor charge before we get to the surface." He looked up the shaft, then over to the oxygen bottles, then back to the shaft again.

"I've got an idea," he murmured.

***

A few calculations on his tablet showed that it would probably work. Liz was skeptical. "Hey, look," Halloran noted, "if we try it, it might not work and we'll be dead. But if we don't try it, we'll be dead anyhow."

That sealed the deal, and the two of them got to work. Halloran retrieved a two-meter length of pipe from his supplies and fitted it to an inline cutoff valve. With an elbow he connected the valve to the pressure regulator on one of the oxygen bottles. He closed the cutoff valve and opened the pressure regulator until the knob spun freely, then he inverted the whole thing and stuck the assembly bottle-upwards into the mine shaft, with the pipe firmly anchored in the tunnel entrance.

"Okay, strap in." Halloran and Liz each clipped their safety straps to the impact guard on the top of the oxygen bottle. "You ready?"

"Scared as hell, but ready," Liz said tightly.

"Hang on to the strap," he told her. "That's what connects you to the rocket. When we get to the top, it'll be my job to time it so we stop flying upward just as we come to the gantry crane. At that moment, you have to grab that crane and hang on for all you're worth. Okay?"

"Got it."

"Okay. Here we go." He opened the cutoff valve all the way.

The oxygen expelled through the pipe turned the oxygen bottle into a rocket booster, and as the assembly started flying upward through the mine shaft, it took them with it. As the bottle gathered speed and shot upward, Halloran was thinking furiously, trying to judge when to shut it off. He had calculated an eighteen-second "burn," but his estimate of the device's thrust was just that—an estimate.

At eighteen seconds by his chronometer, he shut off the valve. The two of them continued to career upward, bouncing off the glassy walls as they went.

"Hey Zane," Liz cried into her suit radio, "what happens if we don't make it up all the way to the top?"

"We fall back down and die," Zane said. They were slowing now, with less than a hundred meters to go, and Halloran could see the gantry crane shining above them, stark and bright in the airless sunlight.

Fifty meters...thirty meters...fifteen meters...five meters...

They were three meters away from the gantry crane when they

stopped their upward momentum and began to fall again. Halloran quickly cracked the cutoff valve open again for a split second, and the added thrust carried them upward. Suddenly the oxygen bottle bounced off the gantry crane, and they were hanging by their hands from the overhead girder.

Halloran hung by one hand, his weight easily managed, and quickly reached the other one over to unclip first Liz's safety strap, then his own. The oxygen bottle fell away from them back down the shaft. He and Liz made their way hand over hand to the side of the hole and safety.

Halloran took a moment to breathe, feel the firm lunar soil under his feet, and take in the bright topside glare of the sun. Liz spoke his thought for him:

"I never thought I'd say this, but even through a helmet visor that sun is beautiful."

Halloran nodded. "It's good to be topside, but we're not out of the woods yet. Let's connect to the satellite and get a report made while we can."

"I wouldn't bother, Halloran," came Colonel Walker's harsh voice over the comm circuit. Both of them turned toward the base airlock to see the colonel himself heading in their direction. Walker was alone, but carrying a vacuum-adapted submachine gun identical to the ones his soldiers had carried.

Halloran reached blindly for the plasma cutter he'd clipped to his belt, but even before he felt that it was gone, he remembered that he had left it at the bottom of the mineshaft. He could hear Liz's gasp over the suit radio. Walker strode up to within ten meters of them and stopped, covering them with the subgun.

Halloran took a breath, expecting any moment to feel the bullets tear through him. He took another breath, then: "If you were planning to kill us, we'd be dead by now. Therefore, what?"

"I hate to waste things, Halloran."

"You couldn't prove it by me."

"Any commander who can't change his plans to adapt on the fly is unworthy of command," the colonel said. "When you first came here I took you for a typical soft civilian. I would hire you to do a job, then send you on your way. Then I took you for an insubordinate pain in the ass—inconvenient, but easily dealt with. Then I found you to be more persistent and resourceful than I had imagined."

"And your point?"

"As it happens," the colonel rasped, "my staff is now two headcount short. And I still need a mining engineer. I want to offer you the chance to join my team. Both of you." He nodded at Liz.

Liz murmured, "He's insane…"

Halloran said, "After you tried to kill us several times over? Why would we want to do that? And why should we trust you?"

"Halloran, you don't understand what's going on here. You think I'm heading up a mission to establish this base for the North American Space Authority—well, I'm not. I'm establishing a base for us."

"Us?" prompted Liz.

"The team. Everyone who is up here is part of the team. Instead of being under command of NASA, we will be an independent entity, our own country. The Republic of Luna."

"But that's impossible," said Halloran. "The moment Earth stops sending shuttles, you're done. They'll starve you out."

"No they won't. The North Americans like rubidium, you see. And lanthanum."

"Not at that price they don't."

"But that's the thing, Halloran. If they don't want it, the Asian Commonwealth will be more than happy to take all we can ship them. Or the Nova Russians, or whoever. You get the picture."

"You're saying that North America would tolerate an outright rebellion for the sake of a little rare earth ore?"

"Not a little," Walker replied. "And not ore. We'll be shipping refined rare-earth metals in bulk quantities starting next month, provided you get this mine back on track. That's enough."

"Enough for what?"

"Enough to tip the balance of power in favor of whoever we send it to."

There was a second in which no one spoke.

"That's the thing about rare earth metals," said Walker. "You've either got them, or you don't. And if you don't, there's a lot of cutting-edge technology you don't have access to, and a lot of research you can't do."

"A lot of advanced weaponry you can't build," Liz supplied.

"That's right. It's a game-changer, and we're in the driver's seat."

"So if we threw in with you, what would the terms be?"

"You work for me, both of you. You get paid something fair, and you get shares of stock. We'll all end up filthy rich by the time it's over, if you care about that."

Halloran laughed. "Filthy rich and nothing to spend it on, living on the moon. Tell me, Colonel, what happened to Jones? I saw the patch on her suit."

Walker's face hardened into a scowl. "Some people are fit to be here, and some aren't," he said. "The moon is a harsh place. It forgives errors even less than I do."

"And Jones wasn't fit."

"I didn't invent Darwin's law, Halloran. I just live by it. So…what'll it be?"

Halloran mused for a moment, considering just how to word his response.

"I don't want to speak for Doctor Barnhart, but as for me, you can…." And Halloran explained in specific anatomical detail an act that he invited the colonel to perform on himself.

"I couldn't have said it better," Liz added.

Walker sighed. "I was hoping you'd throw in with us. Well, with or without you, we'll find a way to move ahead." He gestured with the submachine gun. "Now step to the edge of the hole, and I'll get this over with."

Halloran stepped in front of Liz. "Like hell you will."

Done with talking, Walker began to squeeze the trigger on his submachine gun. Before it fired, his helmet visor erupted outward, showering their suits with gore. Liz and Halloran watched, incredulous, as his body toppled over gracefully in the low gravity, the ruin of his face already freezing in the vacuum.

Behind him, Brantley lowered her weapon. "Sorry, sir. It took me a little longer to get here than I thought it would."

Halloran didn't know what to say at first. Finally, "You knew about his plans all along?"

"Just learned about them the same time you did, sir. Heard it over the comms."

"You were listening in."

"The colonel had shut down monitoring, but I went against orders and turned it back on."

"You disobeyed an order?"

"I was assigned to keep you safe, sir. But now we've got a hell of a lot to explain—I just fragged my commanding officer."

"You'll do fine," said Halloran as he switched off his personal recorder. He tapped the case on his belt. "Get this record in front of a judge, I'm pretty sure things will go your way."

***

Back in the hotel lounge days later, all eyes were on the video feed as the news programs were filled with the story of Halloran and Barnhart and the events that had happened under Colonel Walker's command of Project Green Cheese.

Halloran, down at the end of the bar, took his cigar out of his shirt pocket and considered it appreciatively.

Now I can have this, he thought to himself. *It would have been a shame to waste such a fine cigar.*

He snipped the end off and, out of the corner of his eye, he saw the bartender turn his way.

"Hey, buddy," the bartender began, "if you light that thing...oh." He looked up at the TV screen and back to Halloran. "Never mind."

ABOUT THE AUTHORS

JC Crumpton received his undergraduate degree in English with a Creative Writing Emphasis from the University of Arkansas. He worked seven years for the Morning News of Northwest Arkansas, compiling a list of over 1,000 bylines. His work has appeared in Aoife's Kiss, The Penwood Review, and Saddlebag Dispatches among others. His debut novel *Silence in the Garden* will come out May 2017 from Fleet Press.He currently lives in Northwest Arkansas with his wife and son.

Kevin Findley was raised by a kindly couple in a small town in Kansas. Unfortunately, he misplaced his blue suit and red cape as a child, so he put on a different blue suit after college and served 20 years in the U.S. Air Force. He retired with the rank of Major back in 2009.

For the next three years, he edited websites for a number of commercial businesses before diving into the world of the freelance writer. His first foray into this wonderful, macabre world pf pulp was published in 2015.

Kevin is married with two kids still at home in California and more scattered throughout the U.S. His wife is very happy he finally listened to her and took up writing as something other than a hobby. It keeps him home, makes a few bucks and keeps him out of trouble for the most part.

Lunar Ruse was inspired by Space: 1999 (of course), Buck Rogers and the very normal obsession any young kid had growing up in the height of the space race back in the '60s and '70s.

If you want to tell him how much you loved Zachary Claveaud (or even if you didn't) you can contact him at www.linkedin.com/pub/kevin-findley/35/208/36a/. This is Kevin's second tale with Pro Se. You can expect more from him here and from other corners of the world of Pulp.

Neal Privett lives on a farm somewhere in Tennessee, where he writes furiously, drinks too much coffee, and brews horror pulp in the barn. He is co-host of the local horror hosting show on WEPG television, *Tennessee Macabre*. His stories can be found in several upcoming anthologies from Pro Se, Sirens Call, and Horrified Press, as well as in the magazines Blood Moon Rising, Schlock!, Cheapjack Pulp, Sanitarium, We Belong Dead, and The Horror Zine.

R.J. Holmes lives in Texas with his family. When his son Jason asked him to co-write a book with him he jumped on it. After doing a book and a short story R.J. wanted to write his own stories. Since his favorite genre was sci-fy he decided this would be a good place to start. R.J. has co-written Unknown: War Drums and Unknown: The Well with his son Jason Fedora. Currently R.J. is working on another short story.

Aaron Bittner is a writer by trade and contract pen for hire, most of his output being industrial nonfiction. The first book he ever bought for himself was a short story collection, "Golden Apples of the Sun" by Ray Bradbury. He lives in Rocky Mount, North Carolina with one wife, two of four children, two dogs, and too many cats.